Cryptic Paisley

In This Series

The Margarita Solution

Chiseler with a Glass Jaw

When the Contralto Sings

Stalking the Scratch Man

The Tenacious Goldbrick

Cryptic Paisley

Cryptic Paisley

Cryptic
Paisley

Chester Henry

Published by Dagmar Miura
Los Angeles
www.dagmarmiura.com

Cryptic Paisley

This is a work of fiction. Names, characters, businesses, places, events, and incidents are either the products of the author's imagination or used in a fictitious manner. Any resemblance to actual persons, living or dead, or actual events is purely coincidental.

First published 2021

ISBN: 978-1-956744-12-5

ONE

"I DON'T NEED A HUNDRED sad clown pieces," Celeste said, frowning at him. "Just three or four."

She and Truman were in the Arts District, walking up on an opening event at a storefront gallery for an exhibition titled "A Hundred Sad Clowns." It was still early evening but the sun was long gone, leaving a chill in the air. As they turned the corner onto the block it was obvious which shop was hosting the opening—a cluster of smokers stood out front on the sidewalk and in the gutter, plumes of vapor and smoke rising above them.

There were a lot of people here, Truman saw as they stepped inside, and ran a hand through his thick brown hair as he scanned the room. Celeste pointed out the bar, and they went over to stand in the line.

"One artist generated all these?" he said, gesturing to the array of canvases, lurid close-ups and full-body portraits of clowns in bright saturated colors.

"They're sourced from lots of different artists," Celeste said, raising her voice to be heard over all the conversations. "Sad clowns are a thing right now."

Truman eyed the artworks, the painted faces, every one of them with a frown, or an exaggerated teardrop on the cheek, or both. "Why?"

"I haven't been able to trace it to a single source, but I know an artist who's been doing Chicano sad clowns for a while. Some of the attention might be ironic." She nodded toward the bar. "Get me a red wine. I'm going to do a circuit of the gallery."

Truman watched her step away, pausing briefly in front of each canvas. As she passed by, a tall guy in a gray knit cap checked her out, his gaze following her for a moment. Celeste did look good tonight—she had her dark hair pulled back, and she was still dressed for work, in a houndstooth jacket and maroon pants that flattered her curves.

When Truman got to the front of the line, he found it wasn't really a bar, just a woman in a black vest pouring red from a big wine bottle into little plastic cups. Digging in his pants pocket, he tucked a single in the tip jar and grabbed two of them.

As he stepped out of the throng, Celeste

came back, and he handed her one of the glasses.

"This is all they had."

She slurped at it and scanned the crowd. "Maybe a chianti. Probably cheap, but it's not bad."

"I don't mind clowns," Truman said, waving at the wall, "but I'm not sure I'd want to see one every day. Especially a depressed one."

"You won't have to," she said. "I need these for Mariam."

Celeste worked in the art world, curating shows at a gallery that was a lot more upscale than this one, but she'd started sourcing art for Mariam, an interior decorator, as a side hustle.

From across the room, a woman approached them, her gaze fixed on Celeste. Lanky, with her dark hair piled up on her head, she was wearing an Andean sweater, and a skirt made of pastel-blue parachute fabric, and dock boots.

"Celeste," she said, pronouncing it the way Celeste did, with the clipped Spanish vowels, *se-les-tay*.

Celeste's face lit up when she turned to her, and they exchanged high-pitched greetings and an embrace. Watching them, Truman had to grin at the ritual—Celeste's voice had risen two octaves.

"Yaz, this is Truman," Celeste said, touching his arm. "He's an old friend."

"Not a boyfriend?" she said, giving Truman a subtle once-over.

"Hell, no," he said. "But we do chase the same kinds of guys."

Yaz laughed. "That sounds like trouble. Celeste and I were at college together."

"You studied art history?" Truman said, and sipped his wine.

"I was on a parallel path at the same school. In fine arts. Those were heady days."

"I get it," he said, raising his eyebrows. "California's public universities are the greatest educational achievement in the modern world."

"You're an alumnus too?"

"Just a funder. Through my taxes."

Celeste waved dismissively. "I don't think he actually pays taxes."

"I can't believe you're drinking that ratchet wine," Yaz said. "We should go for a proper drink, and catch up."

"I'm down with that," Celeste said. "I'm getting tired of the clowns."

"That's impossible," Yaz said flatly. "So much beauty concentrated in one place. It's like the Prado up in here."

She chuckled. "Let's just say they make my retinas ache."

"You're not going to buy anything?" Truman said, and gulped the last of his wine.

"In a few days they'll mark down the pieces that don't sell."

He nodded. "So is this next thing women-only?"

"I feel bad," Celeste said. "I invited you out tonight, but it might be boring for you."

"Come with us anyway," Yaz said. "You can drink through all the gossip about people you don't know."

They followed her out to the sidewalk, where Truman inhaled sharply at the blast of cool night air. But it never got that cold in Los Angeles, and he was feeling warm from the wine, so he didn't even bother to zip up his jacket.

Yaz and Celeste spent a minute debating destinations, then agreed on a boisterous little bar on Sixth, and they set off toward it, walking west into the Fashion District. A few blocks later, as Celeste rounded a corner, Yaz stopped.

"I don't want to go this way. I'll get angry."

"This street itself induces that?" Celeste said, her brow furrowing.

Yaz groaned, then took a deep breath. "Let me show you."

Walking down the block, she stopped in front of a shop. Truman glanced up to read the marquee over the door: A TOUCH OF CLASS TEXTILES. Rather than a solid steel shutter, like most of the retailers in the neighborhood, this place had a chrome-plated grid pulled down over the storefront that allowed a view of the display window. It felt less obnoxious, Truman thought, and less prone to getting graffitied, but it looked just as secure.

"That's my paisley," Yaz said, jabbing a finger

at the window. "I designed it."

The centerpiece of the display was a bolt of fabric, partially unrolled and draped on a table, dramatically spotlighted from above.

"I like that it's kind of nonregular," Truman said, stepping closer to peer through the metal grid and study the print. "It's really beautiful."

"It's not supposed to exist in the world," Yaz said, raising her voice. "Not yet. It was stolen from me. I never licensed anyone to use it, but suddenly here it is. I noticed it a few days ago as I was walking by."

"A touch of piracy," Celeste said, gesturing to the marquee, "along with that touch of class."

Yaz scoffed and turned away, stalking up the sidewalk. Truman and Celeste exchanged a glance, and Celeste moved to follow her, but Truman stood there for a minute, studying the paisley. It really was beautiful, dark blue with earthy browns and muted yellows. The pattern actually did repeat, he saw, but it wasn't obvious. Pulling his eyes away, he hustled to catch up.

Yaz and Celeste were silent now, and Yaz's face was hard as they walked into the bar. It was quieter than Truman remembered, with just a handful of sluggish-looking patrons at the tables and no one sitting at the bar, but then it was Monday, and it was still early.

Celeste slid into a booth along the wall, and Yaz waved to the server.

"I didn't know they had table service here,"

Truman said, sliding in beside her.

"They don't when it's busy."

When the server came over, Truman ordered a margarita, and Yaz said, "Same."

"Do you have a decent cab?" Celeste asked the man.

"There's a good one from Paso Robles."

"Hit me." When he'd gone, she turned to Yaz. "So who stole the paisley from you?"

Yaz waved a hand. "I have no idea. I haven't even shown it to that many people. I went into that shop to talk to the owner, but he clammed right up. He won't tell me who's wholesaling it to him."

"I thought you couldn't copyright fashion," Truman said.

"Not the cut of a garment, or the shape of the collar, but prints are definitely copyrightable." She leaned back. "I know it's not worth hiring a lawyer. It just pisses me off that I did all that work and someone can just take it."

The server stepped up and set their drinks on the table.

"Let me get this round," Celeste said, and produced a couple of bills, and slid them across the table.

Once they'd clinked glasses, and Truman had had a gulp of the tart sweet concoction, he eyed Yaz.

"Do you design fabrics for a living?"

"It's one of my many creative pursuits. It

hasn't really generated any income yet."

"It definitely won't if someone else is selling it," Celeste said.

Yaz looked at her drink and swirled the ice. "I guess I get emotional because it's personal to me. Not just that it's my design. Paisley is part of my history. It feels like someone is disrespecting my roots."

"Paisley is from India?" Truman said.

"Before that it came from Persia. My family's Persian."

"Can you trace the rip-off to anyone you showed it to?" he said. "Someone with connections in the industry?"

Yaz looked down. "I put it in a look book that I gave to a lot of people. I printed a hundred copies of it, and most of those are out in the world." She sipped her margarita before she continued. "The weird thing is that the version in the window is good—really good—like whoever saw my printout redrew it in vectors and got it technically very close to the original."

"You could hire Truman to find out who pirated it," Celeste said.

Yaz eyed him. "You do that kind of work?"

"It's my job. I can't promise you anything, but I might be able to find out more than you have."

She waved a hand. "The shopkeeper wouldn't even talk to me. Why would he talk to you?"

"I have other methods."

"You break kneecaps or something?"

Truman laughed. "I know how to buttonhole the saps and make them squeal."

"His guru is a detective handbook from 1936," Celeste said, waving a hand.

Truman shot her a look. "Biff's skills are still valid."

"You've done this kind of thing before?"

"Plenty."

"He has a good success rate," Celeste said.

"What would it cost me?"

"Starting at five hundred a day."

Yaz shook her head. "That's way out of my budget."

"It's cheaper than a lawyer," Celeste said. "It might not take him very long either."

Lifting her glass, Yaz downed her margarita in one gulp, then grimaced and slammed it to the table. "Screw it—let's do it. Stop working when you get to twenty-five hundred."

"Deal," Truman said. "Can I get a copy of that look book?"

"Can we talk about it in the morning? It's too frustrating to focus on it right now."

"Come by my place. It's not far from here. What's your number?"

Truman pulled out his phone and thumb-typed as Yaz recited it, then texted her his address.

"Another round," Celeste said, and waved at the server.

Truman and Yaz ordered margaritas, but Celeste switched to soda water. As promised, Yaz and Celeste caught up on all the gossip about their college peer group. Truman mostly tuned them out, savoring his cocktail, and thought about the paisley.

Eventually they got up and left the bar, parting from Yaz on the sidewalk out front. She leaned in for a double air-kiss with Celeste, then with Truman.

As they walked the few blocks to where Celeste had parked, Truman relished the cool night air. He looped an arm through hers.

"You got me a job."

"I hope it's something you can do," she said, briefly leaning into him.

"I guess we'll find out."

As they walked up on Celeste's little blue car, she stepped into the street, and Truman got in the passenger side. His place was so close he could have walked it, but it was nice to have a ride. Celeste lived farther away, across the river in Boyle Heights.

"Do you want to be here when I meet Yaz?" Truman said, popping the door handle as she pulled up at his place.

"I would, but I've got a whale coming in to the gallery. Keep me in the loop." She pulled away once he'd climbed out.

In the middle of the Fashion District, the hulking brick building had once been a warehouse, now subdivided into a couple of big loft spaces. Truman's was the front half of the upper floor. He let himself in the front door and trotted up the stairs.

It was mostly one big room with a trio of thrift-store sofas arranged at right angles near the entrance. At the far end was a clothes rack, and his bed faced the big tattersall windows, with his desk under them. The only interior walls were a white cube around the bathroom. Celeste's dad had helped him build them. They topped out at eight feet, leaving another eight feet of air to the wooden rafters high above. Eight feet was practical, because two-by-fours and drywall came in that size, and Ernesto said that building the walls up to the rafters would just look weird.

It felt cold as Truman got undressed. With such high ceilings it was impossible to heat the space, and he didn't even try. He climbed under the covers and grabbed the hardback that usually sat on his bedside table, *Eleven Steps to Becoming a Hard-Nosed Detective*, the masterwork of the sagacious Biff Sturgis. Bound in blue cloth, the dust jacket had been lost long before Truman had acquired this copy. He pulled it open and breathed in the satisfying scent of ancient paper.

When he checked the index, there were no references to copyright cases, or to piracy. But he was going to have to interview the shopkeeper at A Touch of Class. He flipped to the section titled "Conducting Interviews" and skimmed through it.

> With most people it's not possible to tell whether
> they're lying to your face. A better tactic than

asking direct questions is to ask a lot of questions in rapid succession. It shouldn't take a chump long to answer—he won't have to think about the truth, but he might slow down if he needs to keep his story straight. You'll know you're being snowed if the details start to contradict themselves.

Even this technique won't work with a cold-blooded lowlife or a crook who has his story well-rehearsed. Another tactic is to interview people in his orbit. Ask the wife what she saw, and the sap he works with, and the barkeep. If the stories all sound the same, it's a lie. If the stories differ, the details that line up are where you'll start to get a glimmer of the truth.

TWO

IN THE MORNING, WITH daylight streaming in the tall windows, Truman forced himself out of the comfort of his bed and hurried across the cold floor to his clothes rack. He pulled on thick socks, and his heavy rust-red jeans, and a blue sweater, then ate some fruit and muesli and made an espresso. This upscale coffee machine was the one luxury he'd invested in when he'd cracked his first case and scored some ready cash.

Stretching out on the sofa that faced the windows, with his back against the armrest, he set the warm cup of java on the table and pulled open his laptop. Once he'd glanced at his email, Truman started to read about copyright in the fashion industry. Lots of stuff couldn't be copyrighted, it seemed, and designers borrowed heavily from one other, and no one resented it because it was expected. Designers made small adjustments to each iteration of a garment, riffing on the previous one and adding new ideas, and the consensus was that everyone benefited from that. It made fashion dynamic, and unpredictable, and fleet-footed, not monolithic and static like industries with more restrictions.

One journalist gave the example of the cartoon mouse that hadn't substantively changed for a hundred years. It was so valuable to its owners that they'd had the feds extend copyright protections for it more than once. As other creations passed into the public domain, the plan for that mouse appeared to be to milk it for all eternity.

But Yaz was right about print designs—they could be copyrighted. Some designers used them like signatures, including one British fashion house that only used one print and put it on absolutely everything.

Truman knew that plaid, he realized, gazing at a rendering of it. He'd seen it many times. It was messed up that he knew what it was now. Every time he saw it from now on he'd subconsciously rank the wearer based on the absurd cost of anything that bore the print. Just reading about this world was turning him into a damn fashion victim.

The doorbell buzzed, and Truman folded his computer closed and jumped up to answer it. He pressed the TALK button and raised his voice.

"Who dat?"

The response was broken by heavy static, and he couldn't parse the words, but he recognized the voice, and buzzed her up. He pulled the door open and listened to the approaching footsteps. When Yaz appeared at the top of the stairs, she was wearing a dark sweater, and had a tan satchel slung over one shoulder, her hair tied up in bright red fabric.

"I love your scarf," he said, as she stepped in.

"It's called a turban." She smiled and reached for his hand.

Truman briefly grasped it, even though he hated doing that, and now he was going to have to wash his hands without it being obvious.

"There's such good light in here," she said, looking around. "So much air."

"It used to be a warehouse. I think the high windows were for the free lighting."

"It feels cold, though."

"That's the downside. It's impossible to get warm in here in winter. Do you want a soda, or an espresso?"

"Coffee me," she said.

Truman stepped over to the kitchen sink and washed his hands, then started the espresso machine.

"So how do you know Celeste?" Yaz called to him. She wandered over by the bathroom and poked her head inside.

"From high school. She would have been here today but she had a whale coming in to the gallery."

"What's a whale?"

"A big spender."

"I've seen the price list for some of the shows she's curated. Big spenders are the only ones who can afford that place."

Yaz walked back toward the kitchen counter, and Truman handed her a little demitasse cup of steaming java.

"It's amazing what people do with their money, isn't it?" he said.

"You're definitely not in the art world. Creative people are grateful when anyone wants to pay for the work."

"Let's sit," Truman said, and nodded toward the sofas, and followed her over with his own coffee in hand.

Yaz sat on the most comfortable sofa, the purple one against the wall, and Truman sat adjacent, setting his cup on the coffee table.

"One time her gallery had an exhibit of these metal sheets with scorch marks on them," Truman said, leaning back. "They weren't even framed. I told Celeste, 'One trip to the junkyard and ten minutes with a blowtorch and I could make that.' She said, 'But you didn't.'"

"Exactly." Yaz sipped at the little cup. "What really matters is the idea, not the execution. And someone else had the idea."

"No judgment," he said, and waved a hand. "I know she loves all that stuff. The creativity."

"So is it true that you and Celeste chase the

same guys?"

He chuckled. "Back in high school, definitely. Not so much lately."

Yaz flipped open her satchel and pulled out a slender sheaf of letter paper, stapled at the corner. "This is my look book."

Truman flipped through the pages, each one with a color rendition of a print. He paused at the one they'd seen in the shop window. It was the only paisley among the dozen or so plaids and repeating prints. The last page had Yaz's name and contact details.

"These are great designs. Innovative, I'd say."

"Usually you attach fabric swatches, but I haven't had any of these manufactured yet."

"Do you have a list of the people you emailed this to?"

"I didn't send it out electronically. I wanted it to be a physical object. I took it to a fabric trade show."

Truman set the book on the table and sat back. "Tell me about the show."

"It's at the Mart every year. Most fabrics are milled in East and Southeast Asia, right, so lots of the companies that attend are from there, or they're repping fabricators from there. People like me go to make connections with manufacturers."

"The manufacturers are there to acquire new designs?"

"Some of them are up for that," she said, and sipped her coffee. "Mostly they're there to connect with clothing designers or local factories who'll buy fabric."

"Do you have a list of the fabricators you gave the look book to?"

"I got some business cards, but I gave it to so many people. I have no idea who most of them were."

"So it sounds like tracking down the pirate through the look book is going to be impossible. Did you distribute an image of the fabric in other ways? Social media, journalists, something like that?"

"The only version of it is in the look book. Otherwise it's just on my computer." She sighed. "It's hopeless, isn't it."

Truman met her gaze. "We know someone is manufacturing the paisley. I'll start with that fabric store. Who did you talk to there?"

"He said he was the owner. An Asian guy with longish gray hair." She gestured vaguely below her ear. "I don't remember his name. He totally stonewalled me."

"What did he say, exactly?"

She looked away. "I have to admit I wasn't in a calm frame of mind when I went in there. I accused him of piracy, and I demanded to know where he got the fabric."

"And he wouldn't tell you."

"He told me to get the hell out of his place or he'd call the cops."

"Maybe I can try a different approach."

"I can attest that yelling at the guy didn't work." She sat up. "Do you need some cash up front?"

"We'll get to that later," Truman said. "I might call you with more questions."

Yaz rose and pulled her satchel onto her shoulder, and Truman followed her to the door.

"Thanks for doing this."

Truman nodded. "I'll do what I can."

———•———

AT THE GALLERY, CELESTE unlocked the door to the street and then settled in at the front desk. The building had once been a factory for light industry, with narrow windows just below the high ceilings. The cavernous space was ideal to repurpose to display art, and in this neighborhood, dozens of similar structures had been. A flight of metal stairs, original to the building but more recently sandblasted and painted bright blue, led up to a mezzanine level with a pair of offices. In its original incarnation they were probably for the shop foreman and the payroll clerk, but now they were for Celeste and for Saffron, the gallery owner.

Celeste hadn't bothered to go up there yet today, as the office windows were dark, which meant Saffron wasn't in yet. Celeste didn't use her own office much, preferring the front desk, where she could keep an eye on walk-ins. Not that there were many of those—Saffron didn't really advertise, and didn't worry about keeping the doors open for regular hours. The merchandise was big-ticket artworks, so serious clients made appointments.

Once she'd sifted through the mail, Celeste checked the office voice mail, but there wasn't any. She'd dressed up to meet her client today, a sharp blue jacket over a low-cut blouse, and the damn jacket was a little tight in the shoulders. Despite that mild annoyance, she felt sluggish, and gray, like the hazy winter morning.

Maybe she could speed things up a little to match her snappy look. Digging in her handbag, she found a Ritalin tab, and popped it, crunching it between her teeth. She checked the clock on her computer screen. Soon the colors in the artworks would grow more vivid, her mind would focus more easily, and she'd catch up to the speed the rest of the world was already running at.

THREE

After Yaz left, Truman spent some time on the sofa making notes on his laptop. Once he had all the details straight in his mind, he pulled on his shoes, and trotted down to the street, and walked over to A Touch of Class Textiles, assuming his rapid commuter pace. It was in the same neighborhood, just a few minutes' walk.

The steel mesh was rolled up today, revealing the display window, and he paused for a moment to look. The paisley was just as eye-catching in broad daylight. Next to the window, taped inside the glass door, was a red-and-black sign that said HELP WANTED. Walking over here, Truman had formulated a plan to identify the owner and start with an interview, but maybe this was another way in.

He stepped inside and looked the place over. Hundreds of bolts of fabric were stacked in deep bins that ran floor to ceiling. A cutting table dominated the center of the room, haphazardly strewn with more bolts, and a service counter ran along the side, with a doorway at the far end leading into the back.

From behind the counter the clerk greeted him, and Truman stepped toward her. In her fifties, maybe, with her dark hair in a tight bundle, she looked to be Latina, and had that air of competence people got from doing the same job over the long term. As he got closer he saw that her name tag read BETTY.

"I noticed the help-wanted sign," Truman said.

"Do you have retail experience?"

"I've worked as a tour guide," he said, holding her gaze, "so I have lots of customer-service experience. Plus excellent people skills."

"That's not as important as selling," she said, looking him over. "Do you know how to sell stuff?"

With a dramatic flourish, Truman gestured to a bolt of fabric that was leaning against the counter. "On your left is a glamorous roll of cotton twill, sturdy and elegant and worn by all the beautiful people up and down the West Coast this season."

"That's polyester," Betty said. "There's nothing glamorous about it."

"But you get the idea."

"Mainly that you have a lot to learn." Her brow furrowed. "My instinct is to say you're not qualified, but I'll see if the boss has time to interview you. There's a labor shortage right now. We're scraping the bottom of the barrel."

Truman raised his eyebrows. "Is there a labor shortage, or is it a wage shortage?"

"Great," she said flatly. "This one's a pinko."

"What does the job pay, anyway?"

"Let's not get ahead of ourselves. What's your name?"

He briefly considered giving her a pseudonym, but he'd probably need to use his real name anyway if they were going to pay him on the books. "It's Truman," he said, and watched as she stepped through the doorway into the back.

As he waited he glanced around the shop. It was dead quiet in here, he realized. All the fabric absorbed any ambient sound.

Betty came back out and lifted the gate in the counter, waving him through, and then led him into the office. It was a tight space, and windowless, containing a desk piled with paperwork and thick fabric-sample books. A couple of bolts of fabric were propped in the far corner, bowed and sagging under their own weight.

The man behind the desk sat up. This had to be who Yaz had met. In his sixties, maybe, his thin gray hair fell below his ears. He was wearing a gray suit without a necktie.

"Shen Jun is the owner of the business," Betty said. "This is Truman."

Shen Jun half stood and reached across the desk, giving him a firm handshake.

"Sit," he said, as Betty stepped out and closed the door behind her.

Truman lifted a stack of file folders from the lone guest chair and set them on top of a similar pile on the edge of the desktop. As he sat, he absently wiped his palm on his jeans, intent on dislodging as much of Shen Jun's biome as possible.

"Mr. Truman," he said.

"It's just Truman."

"Isn't that your surname?"

He had a slight accent, Truman realized. "My surname is Boudreaux."

Shen Jun huffed. "So complicated. Chinese names are so simple. My whole name is two syllables."

"But for a nonnative speaker to pronounce it properly is a very steep hill to climb."

"That's actually true." He chuckled. "Where was your last job?"

"I worked as a tour guide, then I worked the front desk at an art gallery near here." That was a bald-faced lie. It was Celeste's job, but she'd back him up if Shen Jun called to check.

"So what would you do if a customer came in and asked you, 'What's the difference between rayon and nylon?'"

"Well, I'd know they weren't a serious client. Definitely not a designer or a manufacturer. Not knowing the basics means they're more like a hobbyist who'd only buy small quantities. I wouldn't invest too much time in them."

"What specific answer would you give?"

Truman frowned, trying to remember what those fabrics were like. "They're for different purposes," he said finally. "Nylon is less breathable and more durable. It's for jackets and swimwear."

"That's actually a good answer." Shen Jun nodded. "What would you do if someone came in and asked for twenty yards of vintage polyester?"

"If I hadn't figured out where those rolls were stored, I'd ask Betty to point them out."

"What if you knew what the poly was, but you didn't know how old it was?"

"If it looked classic, I'd tell them it was vintage regardless." Truman spread his palms. "Vintage is a broad term, right, not a precise definition. Nobody's going to sue the shop for misunderstanding the meaning of that word."

He sat up. "What would you do if someone came in and asked to use the restroom?"

Truman raised his eyebrows. "Do you let people use the restroom?"

"Employees only."

"I'd say we don't have a public restroom. If they wouldn't leave, I'd go out on the street and flag down one of those bicycle security guards that the local business association employs. They always seem to be around. If one of them wasn't in sight, I'd call the cops."

Shen Jun nodded firmly. "Another good answer." He reached down and rolled open a desk drawer, and dug around, and handed a sheet of paper across to him.

It was a basic tax form, Truman saw, asking for just his name and Social Security number.

"Can you start tomorrow?" Shen Jun said.

"If Betty will have me. She was a little dubious."

"I do the hiring. We open at eight."

Truman took a minute to fill out the form and sign it, then rose, and thanked Shen Jun before he walked out. As he stepped out from behind the counter he saw that Betty was across the shop, halfway up a rolling ladder, pulling a bolt of fabric out of a high bin. A guy in a shiny gray suit with slicked-back hair stood nearby, hands on his hips.

"See you tomorrow," Truman called to her, and not waiting for a response, walked out to the street.

Celeste's gallery was a reasonable walk from here, east in the Arts District, and he set off in that direction. Eight in the morning seemed early. It must be an industry thing. The film industry worked like that too—when they were shooting, everybody was at work by dawn, and home by early afternoon.

He walked up on the long white facade with the chic metal letters that spelled out SAFFRON

SWATI GALLERY and stepped inside. Celeste was with her whale, standing at a canvas half-way along the wall. The woman looked coastal Orange County, with a money haircut, and wool pants, and chunky heels. The bag slung over her shoulder bore a blingy designer logo.

Truman wandered over to the wall, far enough from them that they didn't even glance at him, and stared absently at a painting. Celeste didn't have background music on, so he could easily eavesdrop on their conversation. Her sales mack was always entertaining.

"All these neon colors," the woman was saying. "Is this a thing right now?"

"It seems to be a trend we've identified. It might have enduring power. It also could be fleeting."

"Does it have a name?"

"I'm calling it vibrant semi-abstract," Celeste said. "Personally I've met a dozen people in town who are doing it. They're incorporating each other's ideas. That's often a sign of an emerging trend."

"How many artists are represented in this show?"

"I'm working with four right now. I can get you a bio sheet."

The woman took a step back and eyed the adjacent painting. "It's just so hard to justify it as an investment if you're not certain it'll last."

"I understand that. It's like a risky stock.

If you drop a hundred grand on a few of these pieces, they could lose value, or they might be worth ten times that next year." Celeste waved a hand. "I can't make any promises. No one can predict the future."

The woman tittered and touched her arm. "I wish you could."

"My personal sense of it is that this is happening. That's why we've set up the show."

"Give me a number."

"You mean the likelihood that it'll appreciate?" Celeste pursed her lips. "Sixty percent," she said finally. "You could be conservative and just take a couple of pieces. That would minimize your exposure."

She sighed. "But then I might miss out."

"The other thing to think about is that if they lose value, would you be able to look at them on your walls?"

"No question." She waved her arm. "This stuff is gorgeous. So upbeat."

"Let me get you some information about the artists."

Celeste strode over to the glass-topped desk that stood near the front entrance, her heels echoing on the concrete floor, raising her eyebrows as she glanced at Truman. She grabbed some paperwork, and a few minutes later the woman had thanked her and left.

Truman waited for Celeste to sit behind the desk before he dropped into the chair in front of it.

"You were being awfully straight with Newport."

"If she was buying it just to look at it, I would have given her the hard sell. She's an investor. I'm not going to hype the stuff without a caveat."

Truman glanced at the walls. "To me it looks like cheap mass-produced art from the eighties. Is this stuff really going to be important?"

"I'm almost certain it will. I just didn't want to get too enthusiastic about it with Newport."

"Like you said, no one can predict the future."

"Even so, I think she'll be back."

"So I just got a job," Truman said, languorously waving a hand.

Celeste frowned. "You're already working for Yaz."

"It's part of her case. I start tomorrow in that fabric store. I figure it'll give me a chance to poke around and find out where that bolt of paisley came from." He told her how he'd found the help-wanted sign in the door, and talked to Betty, and the interview with Shen Jun.

"What are they paying you?" Celeste said.

"It's minimum wage."

"With no commission? In this economy, that's a rip-off."

"It doesn't matter. I don't plan on being there very long."

"Well, mazel tov. It feels like drinks are in order."

"Do you want to go to that place with the view?"

"I'll swing by your place after I close up."

He rose. "Deal."

————·————

WHEN TRUMAN GOT BACK to his loft, he grabbed the Biff Sturgis book from his bedside table and took it over to the sofas. Biff had advice about working undercover, he remembered, and he wanted to brush up on it, as he hadn't done a lot of that. Just reading Biff usually gave him the confidence to go out and do the work.

> Going undercover, the easiest way to get caught is to dress wrong. Clothes make the man, so if you're going to be running a shovel, put on the coveralls. If your female operative is slinging hash in a chophouse, make sure she's not wearing her diamonds—that ice will stick out like a redheaded stepchild. The easiest way to go wrong is the shoes. Ditch diggers and bricklayers don't wear glossy polished derbies. Borrow a pair of boots from the super in your building, or trade for a day with the sap who mans the elevator.

Gazing up at the windows for a minute, staring absently at the slice of pale-blue sky, Truman thought it over. He wasn't going to need to wear someone else's shoes, but it was probably a good idea to dress low-key.

Later, his phone buzzed in his pants, and he pulled it out to check. It was a text from Celeste:

> I'm downstairs.

He didn't need to change for a casual bar, he decided, and pulled on his shoes, and locked up, and trotted down to the street. Celeste's little blue car was parked at the curb, engine running, and he pulled open the passenger door.

"You're still dressed for work," he said, climbing in. "I should have put on a decent shirt."

"The rusty jeans are fine. I'm the one who'll be inappropriately dressed." She checked the side mirror as she pulled into the street.

"It's fine to be a little overdressed. Not so much the other way around."

"Lo these many years," Celeste said, "I've just had to accept that I outclass my peers."

Truman had to chuckle at that.

It was just a few minutes' drive to the Historic Core, and Celeste found a street space and backed in. The bar was on the second floor, and they climbed the outdoor stairs and went inside. It felt busy for a Tuesday, with all the tables and barstools occupied, but then this place was always busy.

Truman squeezed up to the bar, and caught the bartender's eye, and ordered a margarita and a gin and tonic.

"There are some hot guys here," Celeste said, taking the highball from him. "Do they seem to be getting younger?"

Nearby, a couple of guys vacated a tall table next to the window, and she hustled over to claim it, perching on the chair. There was a view over

31

the street from here, but mostly they enjoyed the music and watched the crowd.

As it got busier, a couple of guys stood close to their table, waving their hands as they talked. Celeste subtly nodded to one of them.

"Is it time to present the irresistible dichotomy?"

Truman looked him over, admiring the fit of his pants, and his pecs under his shirt.

"Totally," he said. "What's with the epaulets? Is he a cop?"

"You wish. It looks like a boy scout shirt before the badges get sewn on."

The irresistible dichotomy was the choice between the two of them—theoretically any available man would have to choose one or the other, as they were both hot. In practice it didn't usually work, but once in a while one of them would score a make-out session with the ploy.

A minute later one of the pair stepped away, and the one Celeste had pointed out was momentarily on his own. When he turned to look out the windows, Truman leaned toward him, raising his voice to be heard over the music.

"I like your shirt."

"We both do," Celeste said. "In equal amounts."

Looking from Truman to her, he laughed. "Does that mean you're both flirting with me?"

"It's an either-or situation," Celeste said.

His eyebrows shot up. "Does that usually work?"

"With two perfect specimens," Truman said, waving his arm, "how could it not work? It's just science."

"I'm no scientist," he said. "I'm going to catch up with my friends. Have fun, you two."

"I think that really was a scout uniform," Celeste said, watching him go.

"How messed up is it that he doesn't believe in science?"

"That is messed up." She hoisted her glass and tipped it toward him. "We probably just dodged a bullet."

When they'd finished their drinks, Truman leaned across the table.

"I need to get up early. I don't want my eyes to be puffy."

She laughed. "It's retail, not a modeling gig. Nobody is going to care. But we can go."

As they walked down to the street, the brisk evening air felt like a jolt after the sweaty bar.

"Damn, it's cold," Truman muttered.

"It feels good, though. It'll wake me up to drive home."

FOUR

Truman's alarm went off early, and he scrabbled for his phone to turn it off, then sat up so that he wouldn't fall back to sleep, gingerly resting his feet on the cold concrete floor. It really sucked to have a deadline at this time of day.

Black chinos and a black turtleneck, he decided, flicking through his clothes rack. These pants didn't highlight his butt or his leg muscles, but that wasn't the point today. Once he was dressed he slung on his backpack and went down to the street. It felt warmer out here than it had in his place, and he walked fast to warm up. When he got to A Touch of Class, he found the mesh security grate rolled up and the door unlocked. The help-wanted notice was gone. That seemed like a good sign.

Betty was at the cutting table when he stepped in, and she turned to look him over. "You're certainly not going to detract from the fabrics today."

"I figured it was winter, and it wouldn't be that warm in here with the high ceiling," Truman said. "Is there a dress code or something?"

"Shen Jun doesn't like to see too much skin."

"I'm glad I didn't wear a strappy crop top and booty shorts."

She frowned. "You can hang your jacket and your bag in the hallway next to the restroom. We don't have lockers."

Truman wasn't wearing a jacket, but he didn't argue, and went to the hallway in the back, and hung his bag on one of the old-school brass hooks. When he walked back onto the shop floor, Betty waved him over to the counter. She handed him a name tag, with TRUMAN printed in black block letters. It had a safety pin glued to the back, and he spent a minute positioning it on his chest and pinning it to his sweater. Arms folded, Betty stood watching him.

"It's drooping," she said, eyeing it. "With that material it needs backing." She stooped behind the counter for a moment and rose again with a swatch of red fabric in hand. "Lift your sweater." She stepped close to him as she folded it into a small pad.

Truman pulled it up to expose his belly, feeling his face heat up, a little embarrassed that he wasn't wearing a shirt underneath. Betty seemed unconcerned, and unpinned the name tag, and added the folded fabric to the underside. Finally she had it fastened, and Truman pulled his sweater down.

"That's more like it," she said.

It actually did look a lot better, he had to admit.

"So today I'll show you the ropes," Betty said. "First is the computer."

Truman lifted the gate in the counter and stepped in, standing next to her as she clacked at the keyboard. There were no stools here, he realized. He'd heard people say that about retail, that you were always on your feet.

Betty showed him how to charge for the fabric by the yard, and where to enter the product number.

"What if there's no product number?" he said.

"You can ask me. But everything has a product number. It's always written inside the core."

"The core?"

"The cardboard tube that the bolt is wrapped around. Look inside the end of the tube."

She grabbed the end of a bolt that was leaning against the counter, and when Truman peered into the core, sure enough, there was a label with a number printed on it.

"The first three digits indicate the type of fabric," she went on, "like cotton or polyester. You can use those to reshelve the bolts."

Beckoning him to follow, she stepped out

through the gate in the counter and pointed to the shelves.

"This wall is cotton, and over here is rayon, and nylon, and poly. These are the stretch fabrics."

Following her, Truman felt some of them, running the material between his fingers.

"What's the stretchy stuff made of?" he said.

"All sorts of things. The give usually comes from a small percentage of neoprene."

"If someone asks, how do I know what it's made of?" Truman said. "And how can I find out who the manufacturer is?"

"Type the product number into the computer, and click on 'Details,' and it'll tell you the exact composition." She met his gaze. "Don't tell customers the manufacturer's name. They don't need to know that."

"So I should just say I don't know?"

"The product database doesn't always list the manufacturer anyway. You can tell customers the country of origin. That always comes up on the screen." She waved to the cutting table. "Let me show you how to run the fabric cutter."

Just a few inches high, it was a mechanical device that spanned the width of the table, Truman saw. Betty lifted a bolt of pale blue gingham into the groove on one side of it, and unspooled a few inches of fabric, tucking it under the machine. She smoothed it out, and straightened the edge, then pulled a lever that lowered the device until it was touching the surface. When she pressed the red button on the top, he heard a soft mechanical metal-on-metal sound as the cutting head rapidly ran the width of the machine, severing a narrow strip of the gingham.

"Sweet," Truman said.

"It used to be a lot more work. We did it with shears." She gathered up the little strip and dropped it into a basket under the table. "Don't let customers unroll the bolts. They can just fold out the corner. That's enough for them to get a sense of it. Otherwise you'll spend your whole day rerolling fabric."

"What do you know about that paisley in the display window?" Truman said, following her back toward the counter. "It's really beautiful."

"If someone wants some, that's the only roll. Just grab it from the display."

"Where does it come from?"

"No idea. We have lots of suppliers. Shen Jun handles that."

They both looked to the front door as it swung open. A guy with a khaki jacket and thick black hair stepped in and called out a greeting.

"Stay close," Betty said, under her breath, "and watch what I do, but keep your mouth shut."

She was definitely taking this too seriously, Truman thought, following her toward the guy.

He spent the day shadowing her, learning the process, absorbing her sales technique, even though it wasn't especially arcane. Betty had him run the fabric cutter once, supervising as he set up the bolt and measured the purchase, and he rang up a couple of her sales.

Shen Jun came in around ten and disappeared into the back office. Once or twice Truman noticed that he came out to stand at the counter when Truman was talking with a customer.

Later in the day a woman walked in from the street, wearing a long gray coat and carrying a folded umbrella.

"You handle her," Betty said quietly.

Truman stepped around the counter. "Is it raining out?" he asked her.

"It's supposed to, later on."

"Nice. That never happens."

"I like the rain," she said. "It washes all the human excrement into the storm sewers. A rare chance to freshen everything up."

"It's funny how low the bar is these days in this neighborhood. So what can I help you with?"

The woman asked to see some cotton, and looked at a couple of bolts, but didn't wind up buying anything. Truman could feel Betty's eyes on him during the entire interaction. Hopefully he was gaining her confidence.

At five Betty went over to the entrance and flipped the deadbolt on the door. She didn't offer to show him how to lock up, or give him keys. That was a deeper level of trust, he knew, and it might be a while before they wanted him to do it. That was fine with Truman.

"I'm going to cash out," Betty said. "You can

learn that another day."

"I'll head out, then," he said, and grabbed his bag from the hook in the hallway.

On the walk home, his stomach was grumbling, so he stopped at a taco cart to eat. As he handed over the food, the *taquero* grinned at him. *"Gracias, Truman."* Looking down at his chest, he realized he was still wearing his name tag.

Sated by the street food, he felt drowsy, and once he got up to his loft he stretched out on the bed. Just as he was starting to doze his phone rang, and he pulled it out of his pants. It was Celeste.

"How was your first day?" she said when he picked up.

"My feet are killing me, and my back aches."

"You'll get used to it."

"I hope not."

"Were you able to do any digging?"

"The head clerk and the owner were both hanging around all day. They were totally watching me the whole time."

"Once they see that you can do the job, they'll leave you alone."

"I can't believe how wiped out I am," he said. "I didn't expect it to be so much actual work."

Once he'd ended the call, he spent some time gazing at his phone, reading about the fabrics and the types of fibers he'd seen in the store. Eventually his eyelids were drooping. He wasn't even sure he'd be able to muster the energy to get up to take his clothes off.

FIVE

O NCE AGAIN THE ALARM sounded way too early. Today Truman dressed more casually, in a plaid shirt and tan chinos. He pocketed his name tag rather than pinning it on. No way was he going to walk the streets broadcasting his identity.

"I remember that shirt," Betty said, when he walked into A Touch of Class. She was wearing a dark brown sweater with a yellow scarf at her neck.

Truman frowned. "I didn't wear it here before."

"I mean the shirt, not you in the shirt. It was in Artémise's summer menswear line three or four seasons ago."

"That makes sense," he said, pulling off his backpack. "I bought it at a thrift store."

"It says a lot about who you are," Betty said,

raising her eyebrows. "Wearing stuff that's four years out of date."

"I guess working for minimum wage, I'm not going to be wearing Artémise's latest couture."

She scoffed. "Artémise doesn't do couture."

Truman walked into the back hallway to hang up his bag.

"Where's your name tag?" Betty called after him.

When he got back to the counter, Truman took a minute to pin it on, using the folded-up fabric swatch the way Betty had so that it wouldn't droop.

A woman walked in from the street, and since Betty seemed engrossed in the computer, Truman stepped toward her. She had a ruddy complexion, with her blond hair tied back, and she was wearing a powder-blue dress shirt.

"What can I help you with?" he said.

"I'm doing a new canine fashion line," she said. "I wanted to look at some rayon."

"You make clothes for dogs?"

She smiled. "That's right."

He stepped over to the stacks with the bolts of rayon and polyester.

"This section is pure rayon, and these are cotton-rayon blends. They're softer. I doubt your clientele will care, though," he said, and met her gaze, "since they're dogs."

"Dogs actually have great fashion sense. They know when they look good."

Truman saw that Shen Jun had come out of his office. He was standing behind the counter, near Betty and the computer, absently leafing through a stack of paper, but clearly listening in.

"These are the lyocell blends," Truman said, and gestured to another set of shelves.

"What's lyocell?"

"It's a kind of rayon, but it has a smaller environmental impact."

She frowned. "Isn't it all just made of crude oil?"

"Rayon is actually renewable. It's made of plant fibers. Scrap wood and agricultural waste."

"Who knew?" She slid a bolt of the lyocell out of its bin. It was a thick plaid in blue and brown. "Can I unroll this one to have a look?"

"I can't let you do that. You can see what it's like from the corner here."

She frowned and ran her hand under the fabric. "I'll need ten yards of this."

"The dogs will love it." Truman pulled the bolt out and carried it to the cutting table. Setting it in the groove, he fed the edge under the cutting machine and pulled a few yards, measuring them with the rule along the edge of the tabletop.

"Wait," the woman said, gazing at the fabric. She felt it, her brow furrowing. "I'm not sure this is the one."

"Do you need to ask a dog?" Truman said, raising his eyebrows. "They're color-blind, you know. I really don't think they'll care."

She scowled. "Just let me look at some others."

As she stepped back to the shelves, Truman rerolled the plaid. She spent some time pulling out other bolts, and finally asked him to cut ten yards of the first one she'd found. Truman unrolled it again, and measured it, and cut it with the machine.

Shen Jun was still behind the counter when he walked over to ring up the sale. Once the woman had left, he met Truman's gaze. "A whispered bad word echoes a hundred miles."

Truman narrowed his eyes. "I didn't use any bad words."

"It means the customer might complain about the service, or tell other people that we're rude. So don't piss off the customers."

"OK."

"If she makes clothes for dogs," Shen Jun said, "when she's in this shop, that's the most brilliant idea you've ever heard."

Truman nodded, feeling his face heating up. "Got it."

———◦———

LATER ON, TRUMAN BRIEFLY pulled out his phone to check the time. It wasn't even eleven yet, despite the fact that his body was telling him he'd already been on his feet way too long. Betty had just made a sale, and was focused on the computer, but he tucked his phone away. He wanted to lean on the counter and look at it, check his email and read the news, but he knew he shouldn't.

The door swung open, and he cracked a smile when he saw that it was Celeste. She was dressed for work, in a chic blue-and-green blouse and black trousers. Truman stepped out from the counter and approached her.

"May I help madam find something specific?"

Pausing near the shelves, Celeste fondled the loose edge of a bolt of fabric, then frowned and studied her fingers, and rubbed them together, as if they were suddenly contaminated. "There's a lot of low-end stuff in here."

"Then madam should feel right at home."

From across the room he heard Betty stifle a laugh. When he glanced toward her, she was headed into the back office.

"Yaz's paisley is still in the window," Celeste said quietly, once Betty was out of sight.

"I can't really redo the decorating. Not yet. I'm hoping I can get into the files soon."

"I wanted to check out your work environment."

"Pure elegance, isn't it?"

"There's actually a lot of great stuff in here," she said, looking around. "So much potential."

———•———

IN THE EARLY AFTERNOON, Shen Jun walked out of his office and headed toward the front door.

"See you tomorrow," he called, and was gone.

"Does he run other businesses or something?" Truman said, eyeing Betty.

"This is his one and only." She stepped around the counter and walked toward the back hallway. "He has a meeting today in San Pedro about some import business. By the time he gets back it'll be after five, so he won't come back here."

"If he's going to Pedro, it must be about stuff coming through the port."

"I'm going for lunch," Betty said, returning with her jacket in hand. It was light gray but with an odd iridescent sheen, green in places and purple in others.

"Where do you go to eat?"

"There's lots of places around," she said, gesturing impatiently. "I'm meeting a friend at that deli in Westlake."

It was a little surprising that she actually had any friends, Truman thought. "Have fun," he called after her.

Lifting the gate in the counter, he went to the display window, and stepped up onto the platform to peer into the cardboard core of the bolt of paisley. The product number wasn't here. Dropping to his knees, he lifted the other end from the floor, leaning down until his head touched the ancient carpet so that he wouldn't have to lift it too much and mess up the display.

The number was printed inside this end, but before he could read it, he heard the door open.

He quickly set the bolt down and sat up to look. It was Betty, staring at him now, her brow knotted.

"You can't just rearrange the window," she said.

"Of course not. I thought the layout looked a little janky, so I was fixing it."

"I set up that display," she snapped. "Leave it alone."

She walked toward the counter and stepped behind it, and Truman got to his feet. Betty dug in a drawer to retrieve something, and tucked it in her bag, then hurried out the front door again, not looking at him but raising a hand to wave as she left.

Pulling out his phone, he waited a few minutes, in case she was going to double back again, then returned to the display window. He lifted the bolt of paisley and read the number in the end of the core, then recited it as he set the bolt down again, and repeated it aloud as he crossed the room, back to the counter, where he typed the number into the computer.

The database had the price for it, and when he clicked "Details," it told him it was a sixty-forty cotton-poly blend, made in South Korea. There was no manufacturer listed.

"Damn it," he muttered.

Glancing toward the entrance, he stepped into Shen Jun's office and pulled on the top drawer of the vertical file cabinet. It was locked. Inconvenient, he told himself, but not insurmountable, and he walked to the hallway where his backpack hung, and dug in the bottom for his set of lock-picking tools. He'd acquired these on the advice of Biff Sturgis, and after quite a bit of practice, he'd cultivated the skill, and had become a competent hook man.

Door locks with multiple cylinders were hardest, and he could usually get those open, given enough time. In comparison the little push-in thumb lock on the file cabinet should be a piece of cake.

It took longer to figure out which of his tools were the right size than it did to actually spring the lock, but once he had them, and fiddled with them for a moment, the cylinder turned, and the lock snapped open.

Briefly poking his head out into the shop, he made sure that no one had come in. Back at the cabinet, he pulled open the top drawer and started to dig through the files. These seemed to be records about customers, not the fabrics. He pushed the drawer closed and heaved on the next one.

Here were the fabrics, a whole drawer about them, but the files didn't seem to be sorted in any discernable way. Each folder contained a few stapled pages with details of the wholesale order, and the supplier, and what it had cost. Each order had a small swatch attached. That made it easy— he didn't have to read anything, and could quickly look through the swatches without even taking the files out of the drawer.

The sound of the front door opening made his heart start to pound. Betty couldn't be back already. Was Shen Jun back from the port? He quickly rolled the drawer closed, then stepped out to the counter. It was the woman who made dog clothes.

"I need twenty yards of the fabric I purchased yesterday," she said.

"Sure." Truman stepped through the gate and crossed the room toward the stacks of rayon. "The dogs liked it?"

She didn't respond to that, and Truman pulled out the bolt, and measured it for her, and rang up the sale. Once she was gone, he went back into Shen Jun's office and pulled open the file drawer again, resuming where he'd left off, quickly flicking through the folders.

"Yes," he said under his breath—this was Yaz's familiar paisley. He pulled out the file and flipped through it. The vendor's name was listed as Euro-rapt Fabrics. Setting it on the grubby linoleum floor, Truman pulled out his phone and photographed the order sheet, and the swatch, and the other pages in the file.

From the shop he heard the front door open again. He quickly gathered up the file and tucked it back in the drawer, then rolled it closed and pressed in the lock before he stepped out to the counter. A forty-something guy with a scrubby beard and his hair in an Afro stood near the cutting table.

"I'd like to see some swimsuit material," he said.

Truman led him over to the section with that kind of fabric, then stepped back as the guy pulled the bolts partway out and fingered the material. He stood nearby, but his thoughts were back in that folder. He'd found it—the supplier who'd sold Shen Jun the bolt of paisley. But was Eurorapt the pirate, or just a middleman?

The customer interrupted his thoughts. "What can you tell me about this fabric?"

Truman stepped over and pointed to the product number in the end of the core. "Let me look it up. Read this number to me when I get to the computer." He went back to the counter, and poked at the keyboard, and called, "Fire away."

Once he'd read out the number, the guy asked, "Does it have Spandex in it?"

"Twenty percent," Truman said, eyeing the screen. "Made in Bangladesh."

"Who's the manufacturer?"

"I don't have that information," Truman said, even though it was right there on the screen.

"Does it come in other colors?"

"What's in the bin is what we've got."

He frowned. "All right. I might be back."

There was almost nothing in the world that Truman could care less about, he thought, watching him walk out. Pulling out his phone, he leaned on the counter, and looked up Eurorapt Fabrics. It was a small business, it seemed, with only one office, unsurprisingly located in this neighborhood, a couple of streets from here.

Tucking his phone away, he went back to the computer, and quickly typed up a letter to Shen Jun, and printed it. The tone was appropriate, he decided, setting the sheet on the counter and reading it over. In the first line he politely resigned, then he thanked him for the opportunity. In the last line he explained that "Regrettably, my temperament is not suited to dealing with retail customers." Digging in a drawer, he found a pen, and signed it, and put it on Shen Jun's chair.

There was no way for him to lock up, and the wait for Betty's return seemed interminable. She'd been gone for hours. He had stuff to do. When she finally stepped in, Truman had his backpack ready, and pulled it on.

"I have to go," he said.

"You get half an hour for lunch," she said, as she pulled off her jacket.

"I won't actually be back."

Betty frowned. "We're still open until five."

"I mean I have to quit. It was nice to meet you."

"Oh, Truman, really?" She gestured helplessly. "Shen Jun will pull his hair out."

"He can't really afford to do that. He's getting a little thin on top." He shrugged and spread his palms. "I left him a note."

Not waiting for a reply, he went out to the street and took a deep breath as he walked away.

SIX

Eurorapt Fabrics was a narrow store-front with no windows, just a blank stucco wall and a solid door with a plaque on it that said simply EURORAPT. It was locked when Truman tried the handle, so he rapped on it, the metal reverberating under his knuckles. A moment later the lock buzzed open.

Inside there were a couple of flashy aluminum desks, and guest chairs upholstered in lime green and orange. A sculpture hung on the wall, little metal panels painted in primary colors, and a potted ficus sat in the corner. The vibe was like a midcentury cocktail lounge.

One of the desks had a big computer monitor on it, and parked behind it was a slightly built guy, around thirty, his black hair slicked back. A little mousy, Truman thought, but still cute. He was wearing a gray shirt with a weird asymmetrical collar. It was probably high fashion. Betty would know the name of the designer.

As Truman stepped in, the guy gave him the once-over. He would definitely know that Truman's shirt was a four-year-old Artémise.

"Can I help you?"

"My name is Truman," he said, and flashed a smile.

"Huck."

"I work at a fabric store that you sell to. A Touch of Class. I wanted to take a look at your other inventory."

Huck's brow furrowed, and concern flickered in his eyes. "That isn't the only kind of product we deal in. Our business is pretty diversified. We're not really focused on fabric right now."

"What do you do besides fabric, Huck?"

He leaned back in his chair and gestured vaguely. "We have a couple of fashion lines."

"And what are those like?"

"Women's wear."

Truman gestured to the closed door in back wall. "You manufacture them here?"

His eyes narrowed. "We outsource production."

The door Truman had pointed to flew open, and a woman stepped in, eyeing him. She was very dark, more like people from Africa than African Americans, and wore a bright yellow dress.

"This is Truman," Huck said. "He works at A

Touch of Class. That's one of our fabric retailers. Truman, this is Alicia."

"Is there a problem with that bolt?" she said.

She wasn't a recent arrival, Truman realized, as she had no accent.

"Not at all. I really like the paisley you sold us. I thought you might have more to show me."

Alicia studied him for a moment. "We usually deal with Shen Jun."

"I'm trying to make myself indispensable over there, so I'm doing the rounds."

Behind her, a man stepped out of the back and greeted him. He was older than the other two, and thick-built, with wiry black hair. His body language was calmer than Alicia's, more deliberate, like he took up more room.

"This is Flavio," Alicia said.

"The shop owner at A Touch of Class usually handles the buying," Flavio said, holding his gaze.

Flavio had an accent, maybe Spanish or Italian. He'd been listening in—that's the only way he could know why Truman was here. Either the walls were extremely thin or he had a video feed. Truman stopped himself from glancing around to check for cameras. He was getting a weird vibe from these people—they were acting like he was some kind of threat. Biff Sturgis would say that was a clear indication that they were up to something.

Truman gestured helplessly. "Shen Jun is a busy guy. He suggested that I talk to some of our vendors."

"I've dealt with a woman over there," Flavio said.

"You must mean Betty."

He nodded. "I can get you some swatches. Do you deal with other suppliers?"

Truman held his gaze. "A few. I'm new at this. I was trying to take over some of the ones the boss hasn't talked to in a while."

Flavio put his hands on his hips. "Can I get your card? I'll give you a call when I pull something together."

"I don't actually have a card. I just started with Shen Jun. Let me write down my number."

Huck rose and handed him a yellow pad and a pencil. Truman set it on the corner of his desk to write.

"Unfortunately I can't invite you in to look at samples right now," Flavio said. "We're swamped. One of our women's lines is in a show tonight. At Stenman's on Wilshire."

Truman handed the pad back to Huck. He knew that building well, as it was architecturally significant. He used to point it out to the tourists when he led bus tours. In the twentieth century it had been a prominent department store.

"Stenman's has been closed for forty years," Truman said.

Flavio laughed, his tone deep. "The building is still there. The people who own it rent it out for filming and events."

Truman nodded. "Filming fees are usually enough to cover the property taxes and the maintenance. It just means the owner doesn't want to do the earthquake retrofit you need for long-term tenants."

"Well, we're using it for a show. I'm surprised you didn't hear about it."

"Shen Jun and Betty may have been invited," Truman said, "but I'm too new to be in the loop."

"You should come anyway," Huck said. "It's a group show. There's some great stuff."

In the periphery Truman saw Flavio shoot him a look, but he held Huck's gaze. "I'd love to. Can I bring a friend?"

"There's no guest list," Huck said. "You can just show up. As long as you don't look homeless or dangerous, they'll let you in."

"I'll look forward to it," he said, and eyed the other two. "It was a pleasure to meet you all."

Truman turned and walked toward the door. As he stepped out to the street, he could feel three pairs of eyes on him.

That had been weird. When he got to the corner, he briefly glanced over his shoulder, just in case, but no one had followed him. Celeste's gallery wasn't far, and he walked east, toward the Arts District.

When he stepped in from the street, the place was empty, as usual, except for Celeste, sitting at her desk.

"Do you want to go to a fashion show tonight?"

he said, dropping into the chair in front of her.

"That depends on so many factors, Truman," she said, leaning back. "My life is like a complex machine with innumerable moving parts."

"I can see how swamped you are with clients up in here," he said, waving at the empty room. He told her about finding the vendor of the bolt of paisley in the files, and quitting the job, and meeting the staff at Eurorapt.

"Do you think they're the pirates?" Celeste said.

"Maybe, or maybe it's someone farther upstream. I didn't feel like I could ask. All three of them were acting squirrely. Like I was a stoolie."

"A what, now?"

"A rat. A narc. Like I was a threat to them."

"You and that book," she said, and chuckled. "So you'll go see their show tonight to find out what they're up to."

"It seems odd that a little company sells fabric and does a fashion line. Does that sound unusual to you?"

"It's definitely not typical of a small business in that industry," Celeste said. "You focus on one thing and do it well. You don't try to do everything."

"The one who invited me, Huck, might have some potential."

"Is he hot?"

"Nerdy hot."

"But you'd do him."

Truman shrugged. "It can't hurt to try."

"You can call it research."

"If you come with me, you can meet them too, and maybe pump them for information. Ask them things that I can't."

"If they have clothes in the show, I bet they're going to be too busy to socialize. But we could scope it out anyway."

He grinned. "Right on."

"Let's see what's being said about this event." She turned to her keyboard. Studying the screen, eventually she said, "It actually looks like fun."

"Are there photos?"

"Not of the clothes. Just the venue and some of the participants. Eurorapt's photo is just their logo. Listen to the way they describe the clothes: 'Eurorapt women's collection invokes imagery that is neither rational nor consequential. The fashion house is based in Los Angeles but transcends the bounds of geographical location and the meaning of time itself. Presenting and dispersing conceptual garments as nonhuman entities through discursive channels, the Eurorapt women's collection enhances the porosity between the wearer and the observer.'"

"They actually wrote that?" Truman demanded. "That makes absolutely no sense."

Celeste chuckled, swiveling her chair to face him. "It's the way people in the art world describe things. In extremely abstract terms. It makes me think it'll be interesting."

"Can you actually parse what they're talking about? I get that clothes are nonhuman entities, but was that ever in question? And how do you transcend time itself?"

"I can't translate it, but when it comes to art shows, there's a direct inverse correlation between how little I understand in the description and how much I enjoy the work."

"So if they explain it clearly, it's usually boring?"

She nodded. "As a general rule."

"It's clothes. How complicated can it be?"

Celeste waved at the walls. "And this is just paint on canvas, but I spend my days spinning stories to unload it on rich folks."

Truman huffed and stood up. "I should go. I have to find something to wear."

"The first rule of fashion shows is not to wear anything that'll outclass the runway models."

He furrowed his brow. "That actually makes a lot of sense. I'll keep it in mind."

"Sweetie—I was joking," she said firmly. "You have nothing to worry about."

Watching him leave, Celeste had to smile. Truman was so earnest sometimes. She wasn't even sure if he got the humor.

After she closed the gallery, she drove home, to her parents' small bungalow on a crowded street just east of the river. There were no vehicles in the driveway, but she pulled into a street spot out front so that Ernesto and María could park there, and she could leave again without moving their cars.

The house was quiet, and she went into her bedroom to get dressed. A black-and-red print skirt, she decided, and a low-cut top. She spent some time doing her evening makeup, but went lighter than if she were going clubbing.

Flipping open the jewelry box on her dresser, she lifted out the tray, and found a Vicodin, and tucked it into her bra. She didn't need it now, but she might if the event was especially obnoxious.

SEVEN

L OCKING UP THE HOUSE again, Celeste went out to her car and drove to Truman's loft, parking at a meter out front. This street was mostly fashion-industry suppliers, so unlike in residential neighborhoods, there was lots of churn in the parking availability. Walking over to the building's front door, she pressed the button labeled BOUDREAUX.

Truman's voice came through the static on the little speaker: "C— on u—," and the lock buzzed open.

At the top of the stairs she found the door to Truman's loft ajar. He was over by his clothes rack in his underpants.

"I'm not sure what to wear," he called to her.

Celeste walked over and flicked through the shirts, stopping at a charcoal-gray satin one with long sleeves.

"How's this?"

"It fits me really well," he said. "But you said I shouldn't outclass the models."

She handed him the hanger loop. "I think you can take that risk. What about those rust-red pants?"

"In the laundry."

"What else do you wear to clubs?"

Truman dug through his pants. "These flatter my butt, but they're a little loud."

Celeste held them up to look at the print. "They're wild." The material was a deep indigo blue with magenta and purple lines running over it in all directions. "Aren't you into this Huck guy? These might be the deciding factor."

"Sold," Truman said, and pulled them on, then spent a minute on his hair in the bathroom mirror.

On the stairs as they were leaving, Truman said, "You look amazing, by the way."

"We both do."

Once they'd climbed into the car, Celeste pulled into the street.

"One of us should try to get backstage," Truman said. "Maybe we can get insight into who makes stuff for Eurorapt."

"You think the manufacturer will be there?"

"Is that how it works?"

"I doubt it," she said, and accelerated up the ramp onto the 10, the little car's engine straining with the effort.

"Nonetheless, we might learn something."

"By 'we,' I get the feeling you want me to do it."

"It is women's wear," Truman said, "and you're basically a woman. You'd stand out less than me."

"I bet there's just as many gay men in that world as women. But the other advantage is that I haven't met the Eurorapt staff. They won't be suspicious of me."

Once they were off the freeway, Celeste took surface streets to the Miracle Mile, and found parking on a side street a few blocks from the erstwhile department store. The building was actually occupied now, Truman saw, with a row of shops along the sidewalk.

"This was the first deco building on the Miracle Mile," he said, "although the lower floors are technically streamline moderne. The architect was the same guy who built the Ahwahnee Hotel in Yosemite."

"I'm not going to tip you for the tour."

Truman chuckled. "Sometimes this was on my bus tours. I only know the broad strokes."

"You know your history, though. I wish you could cash in on that."

"Preach," Truman said. "Do you know how galling it is that there's money to be made in sad clown paintings but not in knowing about this gorgeous building?"

As they crossed the street, he saw that the shops on the ground floor were already closed for the night, as they were daytime businesses—a sandwich place, a shipping store, a coffeehouse.

"That must be the way in," Celeste said, gesturing to a clot of people on the side street, and they walked toward them.

There was no security guard, just people standing around on the sidewalk smoking. The entry door was propped open, but it wasn't very wide and wasn't marked, like it had originally been a fire exit. They stepped inside, where a couple of people were waiting for the elevator, and climbed the stairs instead, at the top emerging into a big open room with columns painted pastel green. A narrow platform—the runway—rose a few feet off the floor, parallel to the windows that looked over the street, but there were no chairs. A crowd of spectators was already standing around.

"This is amazing," Truman said.

"Except that we're not going to be sitting."

"I mean the room. This would have been a retail floor when it was a department store. It hasn't been renovated since it closed. It's like a time capsule."

Celeste looked around. "I'm just seeing peeling paint and old plaster."

"But it's paint and plaster from another time," Truman said, gazing at the pale-blue ceiling. "It looks so 1950s to me."

Celeste nodded toward the end of the catwalk, where it disappeared into a curtain of sparkly gold ribbons hung over a wide arched entrance. "That's where they're setting up."

As they watched, a woman appeared, parting the shimmering ribbons at the base of the platform and stepping out.

"It looks busy back there," Truman said.

"So I should be able to stroll right in."

Truman watched her stride over, walking like she had a purpose, and disappear through the curtain.

The runway ended just a few feet beyond, Celeste saw as she stepped through. A short flight of steps led up to the platform from the floor.

This space was almost the size of the other one. Racks of clothes stood in clusters at the sides of the room, with people fussing with the garments. Several emaciated women stood around in their underwear. Those had to be the models.

Celeste approached a guy in a black jacket with a clipboard and a headset.

"Where's Eurorapt?" she said.

"Do it," he said, not looking at her. He was talking into his mike. Eyeing Celeste, he frowned and gestured impatiently toward the back of the room.

Walking farther in, Celeste scanned the clothes racks, avoiding the people working around them. She stopped when she spotted it—Yaz's familiar paisley, on a hanger with some other garments. A dress, it looked like from here, or maybe a long skirt. She could feel her heart pounding. Dangling like that, formless and half-buried between other garments, made the print look insignificant, an afterthought, cheap.

In front of the rack was a folding table scattered with paper and an open laptop, but no one was sitting there, or standing near the rack. She glanced around the room, debating whether to take a closer look. It wasn't an ideal environment for snooping. Anyone who happened to look over here would see what she was doing.

Before she could make up her mind, a woman walked past her and stepped behind the table. Wearing heavy makeup and a fitted red top with a wide collar, she was so thin that she had to be one of the models.

Celeste took a step away, turning to face the adjacent table, and pulled out her phone, gazing at the screen but not looking at it, instead watching the model in her periphery.

A buff guy with thick black hair walked up to the model and adjusted the collar of the blouse. He was wearing trendy jeans and a dark shirt, but he wasn't the kind of guy Truman would be crushed out on. This had to be the other one, Flavio. Close behind him was a woman in a yellow dress. She was attractive, but not a model, with a real-world figure. Truman had met her as well—Alicia.

The model slapped Flavio's hands away. "It just fits weird."

"If the clothes don't fit you," Flavio said, raising his voice, "you have to fit the clothes. It's not my fault that you gained thirty pounds. I can't find anyone else ten minutes before the show."

That woman was already a size 00, Celeste knew, eyeing her sidelong. No way was she ever thirty pounds lighter than she was now. Not since grade school, at least.

"You bastard," the model snapped. "I have not gained weight. Your factory cut them wrong. It's your fault. I know you were trying to skimp on the silk."

"There's nothing I can do about it now," Flavio said. "Suck in your gut."

The model huffed and turned away from him, fussing with the buttons on the blouse.

"Why are there no mirrors in here?" Flavio demanded.

"Over here," Alicia said. "Come on."

The three of them walked across the room, toward an alcove where a couple of floor mirrors stood. Celeste had just a few seconds to act while their backs were turned. Taking a deep breath, she quickly stepped behind the table to the clothes rack and parted the garments to get a look at the dress made of Yaz's fabric. There was no label in it, and nothing else to indicate where it had come from.

Flicking through the other tops and skirts and dresses, almost none of them had labels, except one—a blouse. The little tag inside the collar was terse:

SO-CAL BOOTY WEAR

MANUFACTURED IN LOS ANGELES

Flavio's voice came from across the room, shouting again. "So lean into it."

Celeste stepped away from the rack, scanning the room. Flavio and Alicia were absorbed in fitting that red top on the model, and no one else seemed to be interested in what Celeste was doing.

Over by the steps onto the runway, the guy with the clipboard and the headset shouted, "Ten minutes."

Celeste walked toward the curtain, and parted the golden ribbons, and went back into the main room. It felt like there were more people here now, and the din of all the conversations was substantial. She strolled along the base of the catwalk until she found Truman, standing with a twinkie-looking guy near the end of it. Both of them were grinning like idiots.

When Truman caught sight of her, he waved her over.

"Huck, this is Celeste, my bestie."

"I hear you have skin in the game," Celeste said.

Huck's brow furrowed. "What?"

"Your clothes are in the show."

"Right. My company's clothes."

"What's the name of the line?"

"Eurorapt Sport," Huck said. "Eurorapt is our company, and tonight we're debuting our sportswear line."

Her brow furrowed. "I got a glimpse of some

of the clothes in the back. They don't really look like they're for exercise."

"In the industry, sportswear means casual clothing," Huck said. "Clothes for actually doing sports is called activewear."

"That's right," Truman said, nodding sagely. "It's a completely different set of fabrics."

Celeste shot him a look. He'd worked in this industry less than two days—he was just cozying up to Huck. But she couldn't fault him for that. Working at the fabric store was his cover.

Alicia walked up to them, briefly resting her hand on Huck's shoulder. Huck introduced her, and as she greeted Celeste, Truman saw a glimmer of something flick through her eyes. Did she recognize Celeste from the back room?

"Are you working with Truman at A Touch of Class?" Alicia said, "or one of the other designers?"

"I'm not in the industry. Tonight I'm just a spectator."

"Don't they need you backstage?" Truman said.

Alicia gestured broadly. "I've done all I can do. Flavio is supervising the fit, but it's in the hands of the models now."

"So what are the trends in your industry this season?" Celeste said.

"In a way fashion has been liberated from trends," Alicia said, her brow furrowing. "Some of the legacy lines still do seasonal collections, but now that everyone can see anything on their screens, the cycle of trends has sped up so much that it's impossible for any one thing to really catch on and become ubiquitous."

"Interesting," Celeste said. "I guess I kind of had a sense of that. Fashion is a free-for-all these days. There aren't really gatekeepers telling us what to wear."

"If you're talking about the magazines," Alicia said, "You're right. They're definitely not in charge anymore."

At that moment the lights grew brighter over the catwalk, and pumping upbeat music suddenly filled the room. An amplified male voice spoke even louder: "Welcome, everyone."

Celeste looked around for the speaker but couldn't spot him. It didn't really matter, she realized.

After a few introductory acknowledgments, the announcer got down to it. "First up is Blue Crantic Streetwear. Let's give it up."

The crowd hooted and clapped, and everyone shifted to focus on the runway. The music changed, and a model appeared from behind the ribboned curtain, stomping her way along the full length of the platform, at the end doing a twirl. When she was almost back to the curtain again, another model appeared. The parade continued that way, one woman at a time displaying an outfit. There were maybe a dozen garments in all. As a collection it seemed a little thin, Celeste thought, but then these were all billed as small local designers.

The announcer named another line, and the music shifted again. Some of the same women as in the first round were modeling the clothes. There were maybe fifteen pieces in this collection.

"It's the middle of winter," Truman said, leaning close. "They must be freezing."

It was true; these garments were billowy summer blouses and dresses.

"It makes sense you'd be designing for summer right now, though," Celeste said. "By the time these are in production, it'll be spring."

Next up was Eurorapt. A model strutted out wearing a billowy top and a skirt, and then one wearing a fitted top with a pair of tattered jeans. After that came the dress made with Yaz's paisley fabric, worn by the woman who'd been arguing with Flavio and Alicia. The dress looked great on her. She was definitely a 00—accusing her of being overweight was tantamount to abuse.

She glanced at Truman, and they exchanged a look.

After the last of the models stepped back through the curtain, the music stopped, and the announcer thanked everyone. It was over, Celeste realized. There had been maybe eight models walk in the Eurorapt collection, with a dozen garments in all.

After the lights fell, and the applause died away, Alicia spoke, to no one in particular, her tone breathy: "We're famous."

Celeste eyed her, and then Huck. He had a

broad smile on his face, his head still bobbing from the music.

The other spectators were moving around now, and talking, the growing conversations filling the room. Flavio appeared from the back and strode toward them.

"How did it look from out here?" he said, eyeing Alicia.

"Letter perfect," she said, and briefly wrapped her arms around his neck, giving him a squeeze.

"The clothes were flawless," Huck said.

Flavio clapped him on the back and eyed Celeste. "Truman—you didn't tell me your girlfriend was a supermodel."

Celeste scoffed. "We're just friends. And I couldn't wear anything that was on that runway tonight."

"It's not about the clothes," Flavio said. "We should all be surrounded by such beauty."

"You can definitely talk the talk," Celeste said. "I'd call that Old World mack."

He laughed. "The bar is open. Let's have a drink."

EIGHT

As they stepped over to the table, Celeste saw that it was just an array of cups of red and white wine set out on a table. At least they weren't charging for it. She took a couple of reds and handed one to Truman.

Huck grabbed a glass and handed it to Alicia, then took one for himself.

As she took it from him, Alicia looked around. "Where did Flavio go?"

"He's networking," Truman said, and pointed to where Flavio was standing in a circle of a few people, talking and waving his arms.

"He's that guy," Huck said.

There was a tray of canapés on another table, Truman saw, and briefly considered snagging a couple before they were gone. But then he saw someone pick one up, and inspect it, and set it back down. No way was he going to ingest whatever germs lived on that person's hands.

"Your collection had some beautiful pieces," Celeste said to Alicia. "Do you fabricate the stuff in-house?"

"We outsource that part, but we use the fabrics we're marketing."

"That paisley dress was stunning. Where did you get the fabric?"

"Truman's shop is selling it," Alicia said, nodding to him.

That was a disingenuous answer, Celeste knew.

Sipping his wine, Truman caught her eye and subtly shrugged. He casually stepped sideways to try to assess who Flavio was talking to. When he turned back, Huck made no secret that he was looking at his butt. Maybe a couple of ounces of wine had lowered his inhibitions.

Huck leaned closer to talk over the noise of the crowd. "Flavio cut it tight. Some of the pieces just came from the factory today, and they fit weird. There wasn't time to have them altered. After you came by, we were trying to get them to look decent on the models. I wanted to scream."

"I could make you scream," Truman said, leaning toward him.

Huck blushed. "You certainly move fast."

That reaction was surprising, Truman thought, studying him. He'd had the impression that Huck was being flirty a minute ago. But maybe the guy was shy.

"Can I get your cell number, at least?" Truman said, pulling out his phone. After Huck recited it, Truman sent him a text. "Now you've got mine too."

Flavio stepped up to them and gestured to the little glass in Huck's hand. "Enough with the booze. You won't be able to drive." He looked to Truman. "Do you and your friend want to go get dinner? There's a diner up the block."

"I'm in," Truman said.

"So tell the women while I hit the latrine." He turned and walked away.

"Maybe we'll ask the women," Truman said, "rather than giving them instructions." He interrupted their conversation with a hand on Celeste's shoulder. "Flavio wants to go up the street to the diner."

"Good idea," Celeste said. "I need to mitigate this merlot."

"Is that what we've been drinking?" Huck said, peering at his glass.

Once they'd ditched the empty glasses, and started toward the top of the stairs, Alicia said, "Where's Flavio?"

"In the restroom," Truman said. "I'm sure he'll catch up."

"Let's wait."

"Have you been working for Flavio for long?" Celeste said.

"We don't work for him," Alicia said. "We work together. Flavio is actually my brother."

"I wouldn't have guessed that," Celeste said. They didn't look at all genetically related, but then that didn't mean anything.

A minute later Flavio appeared.

"What about the clothes?" Alicia demanded.

"Eduardo is going to take them back downtown," he said. "There's nothing to worry about."

Flavio gestured toward the stairs, and they all trooped down to the street, and headed toward the diner. It was dark out already, and the air was chilly.

The diner was in the next block, and Flavio went in first, and soon secured a corner booth. It was a little tight for five people. Truman slid in next to Huck, draping his arm on top of the booth behind him. At such close proximity he could feel the warmth of his thigh through his pants.

Flavio picked up a water glass and hoisted it. "A toast to our success."

He might be a little buzzed, Truman thought, watching him, because he was talking loud.

When the server came by, Truman said, "We haven't even looked at the menus yet."

"It's fine," Flavio said, and waved her closer, and ordered several appetizers for the table. Once she'd stepped away, Truman eyed Celeste. She met his gaze and raised her eyebrows.

"That Blue Crantic collection looked pretty basic," Alicia said.

Celeste turned toward her. "You thought it looked cheap?"

"I mean the construction. It wouldn't be that difficult to put together."

"Blue Crantic is actually using one of our fabrics," Flavio said. "That brown feather print."

They talked about the other lines, and eventually the snacks arrived. Truman reached for an onion ring. At least no one else had groped it first. Once they'd munched for a while, and verbally parsed the rest of the show, Celeste slid out of the booth.

"I should get going."

"Oh, but the night is young," Flavio said.

"I'm working tomorrow."

"So let's have a proper meal. You'll come to our house."

Celeste smoothed the front of her skirt as she stood up. "You and Alicia live together?"

"We all live together," Flavio said. "Let's make it tomorrow night." He jutted his chin at Truman. "Both of you."

"Why not?" she said. "Truman?"

"Sure," he said. "Celeste is my ride, though, so I have to leave now too."

Celeste waited while he slid out of the booth. The metro was nearby, and she knew Truman would be happy to take it downtown, but clearly he didn't want to linger either.

Once he was on his feet, Truman dug out his wad of cash, and peeled off a twenty, and set it on the table. He'd half expected one of them to tell him to keep it, but no one did.

"Until tomorrow," Flavio boomed, as they turned to walk out.

Once they were out on the sidewalk, Truman spoke.

"Did you see anything in the back room?"

"The clothes on a rack. Plus Flavio treating the model like garbage."

"That guy is kind of obnoxious. Ordering food for everyone. Who does that?"

"I also found a label in one of the Eurorapt tops," Celeste said. "Only one of them. It had a tag that said 'Made in Los Angeles by So-Cal Booty Wear.'"

"Right on," Truman said, and squeezed her around the shoulder. "Was it the one with Yaz's fabric?"

"The floppy green one."

"I wonder why that tag? Blouses aren't really about the booty."

"It's probably just the name of the business. Like the Eurorapt crew has nothing to do with Europe."

"Could Flavio be Euro? Italian or Spanish?"

"The accent is wrong. He's from somewhere else. Latin America."

"His look isn't Eurotrash either," Truman said. "He's a dick, but not a flashy one."

They climbed into Celeste's car, and as she got it started, and flicked on the headlights, Truman studied his phone.

"So-Cal Booty Wear is right in the Fashion

District. Six blocks from my place."

"Do you want to go talk to them together?"

"If you have time," he said, and looked up at her.

"Don't act so surprised," she said, and nosed into the street. "I feel invested in this one. Yaz is a friend."

"I can use all the help I can get. Let's go in the morning."

"Did you think there was something weird about their fashion line?"

"There wasn't a lot of clothes. Maybe ten or twelve pieces. But the other lines were the same."

"It's more than that," she said, braking for a red light. "There was no consistency. Two pieces were in one fabric, and all the rest were different fabrics. Some were dark, and others bright, and there were solids and prints. A couple of dresses and tops, and then one skirt, and one pair of pants."

"I guess that is weird. The other designers used just a few repeating fabrics."

"And their stuff was in the same style. At least in the same genre. And balanced between tops and skirts and one-pieces. That's what you expect when it's called a collection. The Eurorapt stuff felt unplanned. Like they found it all at a garage sale."

"Huck said the sportswear line wasn't their main product. Maybe that's why it's scattershot."

"Maybe." She ran a hand through her hair,

pushing it back. "You know, I get the feeling they're kind of into us."

"Big time. It's weird, right? Do you think they're a thrupple?"

"Alicia said Flavio is her brother."

"Seriously?" Truman demanded. "He's got an accent and she doesn't. How does that work?"

"Maybe they grew up in different houses."

"And different countries."

"I get the vibe that Huck is gay. Flavio's definitely not."

"So they're a business tripod, not a romantic tripod," Truman said. "And they all live together."

Celeste laughed as she accelerated onto the freeway. "I'm looking forward to that dinner."

As she took the exit ramp into his neighborhood, Truman waved at the glittering office towers of the Financial District in the distance.

"So we're definitely going directly home?"

"I really am getting tired. It wasn't just an excuse to bail."

"That's what gin is for," he said flatly. "It's a magical wake-up tonic. But I guess I should stick with my early-to-rise thing and just crash."

When she pulled up in front of his building, they exchanged an air kiss, and Truman climbed out.

NINE

WHEN HIS ALARM RANG, Truman killed it and went back to sleep, waking sometime later when the buzzer for the front door sounded.

It had to be Celeste, he knew, and jumped up to buzz her in, and flip open the deadbolt on the door. He hustled over to his clothes rack and pulled on a pair of pants.

"I woke you," Celeste said as she stepped in.

"I was up. I was just making coffee."

"You lie," she said flatly.

"Do you want an espresso?"

She waved a hand. "Set me up."

Truman pulled on a shirt and stepped into a pair of warm socks. As he padded over to the kitchen counter, he looked over her outfit: dark pants and a jacket, with her hair bundled behind her head.

"You dressed up."

"It's called working a look. As in, industry professional." She sat on the purple sofa and crossed her legs.

"It's very professional." Once he'd pulled the espresso, he brought over the two demitasse cups and handed her one, then sat on the adjacent sofa.

"So how do you want to approach So-Cal Booty Wear?" Celeste said, once she'd had a sip of the steaming java.

"We ask for a meeting with the owner."

"Do you think they'll just open their customer list for us?"

Truman pulled out his phone. "Let's figure out what they actually do first." He tapped at it and peered at the screen. "The website says 'specializing in the production of glamorous clothing from couture to large runs.'"

"So it's a manufacturer. I thought maybe it was a fashion line, and that piece belonged to another designer."

"We'll tell them we're launching a line, and ask about other clients, so that we can check the quality of the production. Like asking for a reference."

"That might work," she said, and set her cup down. "I need to know what I'm talking about, though. I should do some reading."

They talked some more about their approach, and worked up a plan. Finally Celeste said, "Can

I use your laptop?"

Truman got up, and went over to grab it from his desk under the windows, and handed it to her. She'd already kicked her shoes off, and stretched out on the sofa, and got into it. After he'd eaten some fruit, Truman spent the time reading too.

"Check the page I just sent you," she said.

Truman pulled it up and read through it. It was a rundown of the steps in the process of bringing clothes from the concept stage into finished products. Eventually Celeste folded the laptop closed and sat up.

"I think I'm ready."

Truman got up too. "Let's roll."

Once he'd pulled on his shoes, and stuffed his laptop into his backpack, he locked up and followed Celeste down to the street. Standing at the edge of the alley that ran beside his building was Beretta, one of the many homeless people who slept in tents back there. He was wearing a heavy khaki-green coat and a knitted cap over his shaggy hair. Truman called out a greeting.

"Hey, sweet cheeks," Beretta said, absently pulling on his beard. "I saw your girlfriend's car. I've been keeping an eye on it."

"I'm not his girlfriend," Celeste said.

"It's going to sit there for a while," Truman said. "Can I ask you to maintain your surveillance?"

Beretta stepped closer. "Funding from President Jackson would allow me to continue the work."

Digging in his pocket, Truman found a fin. "How about Honest Abe?"

Beretta didn't protest, and when he handed over the bill, it quickly disappeared into a pocket.

Once they were walking up the block, Celeste spoke.

"That guy seems so much more lucid than a lot of your homeless neighbors. He's definitely more together than Angel ever was."

"Not all of them are mentally ill and off their meds. The county says it's only about sixty percent."

Celeste scoffed and looped her bag around her opposite shoulder.

When they walked up on the address, it was a long two-story building with several retail tenants on the ground floor. The sign for So-Cal Booty Wear was at the foot of the stairs, with an arrow pointing up.

"That's the same logo as on the tag in that blouse," Celeste said, and they climbed up. She pulled open the door and they stepped inside.

This was definitely a factory, with two long tables for cutting, one of them strewn with manila pattern segments and a bolt of denim. At the side of the room, along the windows, sat sewing machines, mostly idle but a few occupied by workers. The sound of the little motors cycling on and off filled the space. It was one big room with no office in sight, but at one side a man sat at a cluttered desk. He got up when they stepped in. Taller than both of them, he was wearing a pastel-orange sweater and had a precipitous pile of dreadlocks.

"Can I help you?"

"My name is Penelope," Celeste said, "and this is Isaac. We're starting a sportswear line. I've seen some work you've done, and I wanted to talk about production."

He smiled. "As you can see, that's what I do here. I'm Gavin. Come and sit."

Gavin waved at the lone chair next to his desk, then rolled over an armless chair from a sewing table for Truman, and sat down as they did.

"Where did you see my work?"

"A designer called Eurorapt," Celeste said.

His face clouded. "That guy. I wouldn't call him a designer. He didn't even have labels to sew into his clothes. I had to use my own."

"Clothes have to have labels in them?" Celeste said.

"I don't let anything go out the door without a label."

"So if he's not a designer, he's a hobbyist?" Truman said.

Gavin sat back. "I don't work with him a lot. He has me do minimum lots sometimes."

"What are your minimums?" Celeste said.

"It depends. For a straightforward garment, usually ten. More complicated pieces are twenty-five."

"So you're not a regular manufacturer for Eurorapt?"

"They're not a regular line." Gavin spread his palms. "It seems to me like they do things at random. I'd say it's not well thought out."

"Like not having their own labels," Celeste said.

"Exactly. Then there's the issue of knock-offs."

Truman frowned. "What does that mean?"

Gavin pursed his lips. "I shouldn't be gossiping," he said finally. "Where are you with your line?"

"I've got drawings for a dozen pieces," Celeste said. "I'm working with a guy now to get them translated into patterns."

"A pattern grader?"

"That's right. It's hard to find a good one."

"Tell me about it," he said emphatically.

"This one seems to know what he's doing. Once I get the patterns graded, I'll need help from someone like you."

Truman eyed her sidelong. She'd put the morning to good use in learning the lingo. He held up a finger.

"Before we get to that, I want to know more about Eurorapt. We do some business with them. Is there anything we need to be wary of? We kind of need to know."

"Well, I don't judge."

"But you do have concerns."

"I see a lot of lines," Gavin said. "The more high-profile they are, the more carefully they keep their designs under wraps until they're on the market."

"Eurorapt doesn't seem that high-profile," Celeste said.

"Not them—Eurorapt is making the knock-offs. They have patterns ready for copies of high-profile stuff almost as soon as it hits the market."

"That's not really illegal, though," she said. "You can't copyright designs."

"Of course not. But usually the process of copying something takes time. If you want the knock-off to be affordable, you go through an Asian factory. You won't see the knock-offs on sale for four to six months. If people approach me to make knock-offs, they cost a lot more, but they might get something on sale a couple months later." Gavin leaned forward. "But Euro-rapt has brought me patterns the same week that the originals debut."

"That is odd," Truman said. "To move so fast."

Gavin threw up his hands. "But like Penelope said, it's not illegal. The patterns were odd too. They were on the right kind of manila cardstock, but cut weird. Like someone had done it in a hurry, with a pair of scissors, and didn't quite hew to all the lines."

"Patterns are about precision," Celeste said. "You can't do them fast or sloppy."

"Can you tell me what designers they had the jump on?" Truman said.

He groaned. "It feels so gossipy."

"It's not a trade secret, though, right? Lots of

people know about it."

"There's a store on Cahuenga in Hollywood that has its own line. The place is called Feel the Trend. I know Flavio had the same top ready for production the same week. It was this sheer blouse with a V-cut neck and long tails. I refused to manufacture it for him because I was making the original. I couldn't very well be making the copies too."

Truman nodded. "Good to know."

Celeste shifted in her seat. "So what kind of lead time do you need?"

She was sticking to character, Truman realized, and tuned them out so that he could memorize the name of the shop on Cahuenga. Feel the Trend. He repeated it a few times in his head.

Gavin talked more about production, and Celeste asked some technical-sounding questions. Eventually she sat up.

"I'll be in touch when my patterns are ready."

Gavin smiled as he rose, then gave each of them a firm handshake. "Let's do some work."

As they walked out and descended the stairs, Truman was mostly thinking about where he could wash his hands.

"What the hell are those weirdos up to?" Celeste said.

"It's so suspicious, right? We'll have to ask a lot of questions at dinner."

"It sounds like Yaz isn't the only designer they've ripped off."

"I want to check out that shop on Cahuenga that Gavin talked about," Truman said. "I wonder if they know about Eurorapt."

"I should go to the gallery."

"Do you want me to walk you to your car?"

"Just go," she said. "It's not far back to your place, and Beretta is on guard."

"That guy is a scrounge. Do not give him any more money."

———◆———

STRIDING OFF IN THE opposite direction, Truman assumed his rapid commuter pace, heading toward the central library. It was hard to see the squat structure these days, as it was surrounded by skyscrapers, but occasionally he caught a glimpse of its decorated crowning pyramid in the distance. As he'd explained to people on his downtown walking tours, the classical Egyptian elements were inspired by the discovery of Tut-ankhamen's tomb around the time it was built in the 1920s.

Inside the atrium, Truman went down the long escalators to the research floors and found a desk. First he made notes for his report to Yaz, about Eurorapt selling her fabric, and the lone dress made from it in the oddly eclectic collection. He thought about what Gavin had told them, about the rapid knock-offs. Could that be connected to Yaz's work being pirated?

Searching the library's catalog on his laptop,

he found some books about paisley, and read about its history. It aligned with what Yaz had said about its origins being in Persia.

Eventually Truman packed up his bag and went up to the lobby, and out into the little green space in front of the library. It felt warmer out now, and he sat on a bench in the sun, and dug out his phone, and called Yaz. Her voice mail picked up.

"I wanted to give you an update," Truman told the machine. "I'm interviewing people, and I have some leads. I'm close but it's going to take me a few more days. Don't worry about the billing, though. I won't break your budget limit."

Cahuenga was in Hollywood, and Truman went to the metro and rode the rails to Sunset Boulevard, then walked to the trendy retail district. Feel the Trend had a broad storefront with a couple of mannequins set up outside. The clothes on display looked like what they'd seen last night: trendy women's sportswear.

The clerk on the register looked up as Truman approached. He was basically hot, with knobby black hair and a tight T-shirt.

"Can I help you?"

"I'm looking for the owner."

His brow furrowed. "Are you selling something?"

"I'm investigating a fraud case."

"You don't look like a cop."

"I'm not," Truman said, and raised his eyebrows.

"All right. Her name is Rocky. She's somewhere in the back."

Walking farther inside, he scanned the clothes. They had an earthy organic feel, without being too heavy, in tans and greens and batik. There was silver and turquoise jewelry for sale, and scarves, even decorated wooden boxes and tchotchkes, and pillows with little mirrors sewn into them.

He walked past a couple of women digging through a clothes rack, and then a woman on her own, but she had a bag on her shoulder—she didn't work here. Farther back he found her. Standing at a table laden with squat bulky candles, a woman with long dark hair looked up at him and smiled. She was wearing jeans and one of the blouses from the displays.

"Welcome," she said, with the confident air of ownership.

"I'm investigating a copyright infringement case," Truman said, and handed her his business card. "I wanted to ask you about that."

"Who are you working for?" Rocky said, briefly studying the card.

"A designer whose fabric showed up in a shop window without her knowledge."

She nodded. "I get it. There's always people ready to snap up original ideas."

"In this case it's more than just borrowing. It was a precise rendering of a copyrighted design. That's illegal."

"Who sent you here?"

"I talked to Gavin at So-Cal Booty Wear. He mentioned your line."

"I don't buy any local fabrics for my line," Rocky said. "I source them in Southeast Asia."

"Have you ever worked with a company called Eurorapt?" Truman said.

Her brow furrowed, and Truman saw the unmistakable spark of recognition in her eyes. He watched her, seeing the wheels turn, waiting for a response.

A muffled *ding* sounded, and Rocky pulled her phone from her hip pocket and glanced at it.

"Can you help me out with something?"

"It depends," Truman said. "What do you need help with?"

"You don't have to say anything. Just come with me and observe."

"Right now?"

Rocky strode toward the front of the store, and Truman followed.

"Leave your backpack here," she said, stepping behind the register with the clerk and waggling her fingers for it. "It'll be safe."

Truman slipped it off and handed it over, then followed her toward the entrance.

"What are we doing, exactly?" he said, hustling to catch up and walk abreast.

"It won't take long."

"That's not an answer."

"We're already here." She gestured to the

storefront next to hers and pulled open the door.

The interior was under construction, with a pile of lumber under the display window, and power tools on the floor, and a paint-spattered ladder. Toward the back a couple of guys in work clothes were framing a wall. One was handling the two-by-fours, and the other was tapping them with a nail gun that snapped with each contact.

As they stepped inside, a rail-thin man with white hair turned to them. This wasn't a manual laborer, tall and Anglo and wearing dress pants and a puffy dark-orange vest that looked like skiwear. Even from across the room Truman could tell it was ripstop nylon.

"Is this your electrician?" the guy said, jutting his chin toward Truman.

Truman's eyes narrowed. "What's going on?"

"I own this building, chum. You need to go through me if you're going to start messing with the wiring."

"I'm not your chum," Truman said, and Rocky tapped his arm, a tacit exhortation to shut up.

"I pay you plenty," she said to the guy, "and I'm never late. You need to back off."

"And you need to have some respect."

"A hard lease means I can do whatever the hell I want."

He shook his head. "Not if it's a safety issue."

"I'd be happy to get a fire department inspector in here," Rocky said, "and we can all go through what's safe and what's not."

His face clouded. "You'd best mind your own business."

"So stop digging into mine," Rocky snapped.

He turned to Truman, and pointed two fingers at his own eyes, then jabbed one at him: *I'm watching you.*

Truman scowled at him, then realized Rocky had turned to leave, and hustled to follow her out.

Once they were on the sidewalk in the sunshine again, Rocky immediately seemed calmer.

"What the hell was that all about?" Truman demanded.

"Let's go to the coffee place on the corner."

"I'll catch up." He stepped into Feel the Trend and eyed the clerk. "I need my backpack."

His eyes narrowed, but he handed it over. "Where's Rocky?"

"She'll be back soon."

The coffeehouse had big windows facing two streets, and Truman ordered an espresso, then went over to sit with Rocky along the wall.

"I take it that was your landlord," he said as he sat down.

Rocky tucked her hair behind her ear. "We're having a little conflict."

"Why did he think I was doing your wiring?"

"Don't worry about that." She sipped her coffee. "You asked about Eurorapt."

Truman took a breath and mentally shifted gears. "I think you know the company."

"I know they have batik fabrics sometimes.

I've consulted them as a potential source. But I haven't bought from them."

"Have you seen their women's line?"

"I didn't even know they had one. Is it significant?"

"I haven't seen all of it, but someone said one of the pieces looked a lot like your line. Specifically the top with the long tails and V-cut neck."

She shrugged. "Everyone copies everything. It's part of the deal. Did Gavin tell you that?"

"I know he manufactures that piece for you."

"Have you spoken to Flavio about his exchange network?"

Truman frowned. "What's that?"

"He's setting up an exchange for people in the industry so we can pay each other in cryptocurrency. The idea is that if you don't use the U.S. dollar, you can keep the government out of it."

"The government is still going to tax you, whether you work in dollars or not, don't you think?"

"I'm not sure exactly how he's setting it up. He says it'll give small companies financial privacy." She grinned. "My accountant thinks like you do, though. He says I'll still be liable for the taxes."

Truman folded his arms. "Have you given Flavio any money?"

"Not yet. But he's shown me the software."

TEN

At the gallery, Celeste locked the front door, and flipped the sign over to read CLOSED, then strode toward the back exit to the alley. Halfway across the room she paused. Maybe it wouldn't hurt to slow things down. She pulled her bag off her shoulder, and dug around, and found a Vicodin. Biting it in half, she dropped the other half back in an inside pocket.

Once she'd set the alarm, she stepped into the alley, and heaved the heavy fire door closed, and locked it. The security guard that the merchants hired to keep the alley clear of tents and graffiti was slowly cruising past, in a little white car with an orange light bar on top. Celeste waved to him before she climbed into her own vehicle.

A few minutes later she pulled up in front of

Truman's building. When she pressed the button next to his name, the door buzzed open.

"Do we have time for java before we go?" Truman said when she stepped into his loft.

"Not for me. Knock yourself out."

"There's some of those Italian sodas in the icebox," Truman said, and went to turn on the espresso machine.

"The icebox?" She stepped over to the refrigerator, and grabbed one of the sodas, and twisted off the cap. "That sounds like a word straight out of your detective book."

"In Biff's day someone would actually bring a block of ice to your kitchen and put it in the icebox," Truman said, raising his voice over the noise of the coffee machine. "Posing as the ice delivery man was an easy way to infiltrate someone's house. All you needed were coveralls and a pair of ice tongs."

"You should totally buy some of those." Celeste put a hand on her hip and sipped her soda.

"An ice pick was a common household tool. You wouldn't believe how many people got stabbed with those."

"Such practical knowledge for the twenty-first century."

Truman chuckled as he poured the steaming java into a mug and waved her over to the sofas.

"You dressed up," Celeste said as she sat down.

"This is one of the few shirts I own that flatters my body."

"And those are club-night pants. I bet old Biff would call that an intriguing clue. You must be seriously interested in Huck."

Truman sipped his coffee and crossed his legs. "He's a means to gather information."

"A means who flirts back. What did you find out at the shop that Gavin mentioned?"

"Feel the Trend," he said, and told her about meeting Rocky, and what she'd said about Flavio's cryptocurrency plan.

"Whether the banks handle your transactions or someone else does," Celeste said, "you still owe taxes on it. You have to report all income from all sources. It's one of the basic rules."

"That's what I thought too."

"The tax people will know about it the second someone tries to turn it into real money. It doesn't matter that it's not in U.S. dollars."

"It doesn't make sense, right?" Truman waved a hand. "I read a little about it. Working in cryptocurrency doesn't really make you anonymous. Crypto works on a ledger, and part of the point is that anyone can inspect the ledger. So anyone can see the transactions. In those big ransomware attacks, it took the feds a hot minute to figure out who got the payouts."

"So Flavio is promising anonymity, but Rocky doesn't know how it actually works."

"It feels hinky. I hope she doesn't invest with him until she does some research."

"Flavio seems to have a lot of stuff going on.

A renaissance man."

Truman drained his cup and rose. "I'm not sure that's the right word for him."

Once he'd locked up, they walked down the stairs to the street. The last pinky-orange dregs of sunset glowed in the west.

"So where exactly do these people live?" Celeste said, once they'd climbed into her car.

"West Adams," Truman said, and pulled out his phone. "Go down to Jefferson and hang a right."

"Isn't that one of those rough neighborhoods around USC?"

"Huck texted me their address." He peered at the map on his screen. "It can't be far from there."

"They put a big fence around it to keep the rabble at bay," Celeste said, pointing to the heavy steel barrier that fronted the campus. "It's like a little bubble of white privilege surrounded by poor people."

"These neighborhoods aren't that rough anymore. In the nineteenth century it was a wealthy suburb, so there's great housing stock. Lots of it has been neglected, but it's still here."

"So the gentrifiers are moving in and fixing them up."

"A-yup."

When they turned onto the street and looked for house numbers, she saw that they really were stately old structures, with a few newer houses and faded apartment buildings mixed in. Celeste backed into a parking spot, then reached into the backseat to grab a bottle of wine.

"Did they ask you to bring that?" Truman said.

"You can't just show up for dinner empty-handed, you philistine."

"I guess I should be glad somebody has manners."

He watched her for a moment as she climbed out. Celeste's eyelids looked a little heavy. She hadn't got completely clean, he knew, after he'd confronted her about it a while back. Since then even broaching the subject of her drug use risked a blowup, so now wasn't the time. He sighed. Maybe she was just tired.

The house had a small front yard separated from the street by a low fence. The gate hung open, and they stepped through it, and onto the porch, flanked by two columns.

"It's an elegant place," Celeste said. "Is it a Craftsman?"

"This neighborhood is older than that. It would have been a prosperous family's house. Servants quarters and the whole bit. See the carport? Those were originally for horse-drawn carriages."

She rapped on the front door. Truman tried the handle, finding it locked, and Celeste shot him a look.

"What?" he demanded.

At that moment Alicia pulled it open, and

beamed, and welcomed them in.

"This is a great house," Celeste said, and handed her the bottle of wine. "How many bedrooms?"

"Three, but originally there were five. We've repurposed a couple of them."

"You'll have to give us the tour later," Truman said, gesturing to the staircase, made of dark polished wood with an intricately carved newel post.

Concern flitted through her expression. "I hope you're hungry. Let's sit."

Alicia led them into the dining room, just off the foyer. The table that dominated the space was set for five. That was a little surprising, Celeste thought. No chitchat, no drinks first, just straight to the main event.

"If you two could sit at the back," Alicia said, and then took the chair across from Celeste.

Heavy footfalls sounded on the stairs, and Flavio walked into the dining room.

"Don't get up," he boomed, even though neither of them had moved from their chairs. He stood at the end of the table.

"I like your house," Truman said, and they chatted about it for a minute, until Huck stepped in from the other doorway and greeted them.

As the door swung closed on its springs, Truman caught a glimpse of kitchen counters and a refrigerator. Huck was wearing a food-stained butcher's apron, and absently wiped his hands on it.

"We'll start with the soup course," he said, "if we're all ready."

Flavio rolled a finger in the air. "Bring it on, man."

Huck stepped back into the kitchen, and Flavio sat at the head of the table, with Alicia at one elbow and Celeste at the other. Huck brought the soup plates in, two at a time, carefully setting them down. When he joined them, sitting across from Truman, he left his apron on.

"*Buen provecho,*" Flavio said, and started in on the soup. Eyeing Celeste, he said something else in Spanish.

"I know I look like I should speak the language," she said, "but I don't."

Flavio gestured with his spoon. "I'm shocked that it's so easy to lose the connection to your roots."

"I'm still connected to my extended family. We've taken trips to Zacatecas and Durango."

"But without the language, you must miss a lot."

"Where are your people from?" Celeste said.

"Peru. But I'm not a *limeño.* That's who people think of when they think of Peru. They're the *criollos* who've run the country since the beginning."

"If you're not *criollo,* what group do you identify with?"

"I'm *serrano.* It means from the countryside."

"What brought you to LA?" Truman said.

"A beautiful woman."

"I guess that's as good a reason as any to migrate."

Flavio set down his spoon and straightened up. "I love beautiful women. I love to see them look good, and so I love fashion." He eyed Huck and raised his eyebrows.

Huck got up, and collected their soup plates, and carried them into the kitchen.

"Bring a corkscrew," Flavio called after him.

Briefly stepping back into the room, Huck handed it to him, and Flavio went to work opening the wine. He half stood to pour for each of them. When he filled Celeste's glass he held her gaze, a smirk on his face.

She'd noticed the flirting, Truman knew, as Celeste eyed Flavio sidelong as she took a sip, and raised her eyebrows.

"That's good stuff," she said.

She wasn't discouraging him, Truman decided, but she wasn't totally flirting back either. Alicia's reaction caught his eye—her brow furrowed, and she set down her wineglass, and folded her arms. It really did seem odd that they were siblings. She didn't look Latin American, *criollo* or otherwise.

The next course appeared, with Huck carrying plates on his arms like a busboy. As he set Truman's dish in front of him, he saw Huck's thumb was touching the food.

"This is called socca," Flavio said. "It's made with garbanzos. It's from Italy."

"You made it?" Truman asked Huck as he sat down.

"It's a collaboration," Flavio said.

"What's in it besides garbanzos?" Celeste said, eyeing Huck.

"Leeks, and bell peppers, and carrots."

"Why carrots?" Flavio said.

Huck shrugged. "It's not traditional, but we had lots of them."

"I'm loving the carrots," Truman said, waving his fork. "They're cooked perfectly."

"I'm glad." Huck held his gaze for a moment, a trace of a grin on his face, then looked down.

"So, Alicia," Celeste said. "What's your role at Eurorapt?"

"Whatever needs to be done."

"Do you design garments?"

"I'd say I implement garments. I find people to sew from the patterns we have, and I source fabrics, like at Truman's shop. What do you do for work?"

"I'm in the art world. Right now at a gallery."

"You work with artists?"

"Right. I try to identify trends and acquire stuff that'll sell."

"I took some art history," Alicia said. "It's interesting stuff."

"Your acquisitions are one-offs, aren't they?" Flavio said. "The paintings you sell?"

"They're unique artworks," Celeste said. "Not mass produced, if that's what you mean."

"I don't see how you can make any money. If you can't make a thousand copies, you're only ever going to earn on it once."

"True, but I move pieces that are worth a lot, and I build relationships with buyers who come back for more. I just sold a canvas for fifty grand."

"Do you get a cut of that?" Flavio said.

She smiled. "A small cut."

Alicia set her fork down. "So what's hot right now in visual art?"

As Celeste started to explain some of the trends, Truman could feel Flavio's eyes on him. It made the hair on the back of his neck stand up. It felt like he was being assessed, or evaluated, like someone studying the rack of paint chips at the hardware store. Avoiding his gaze, Truman focused on eating around the spot where Huck's thumb had touched his dinner.

"So how much does Shen Jun pay you?" Flavio said.

"Not enough, of course," Truman said, looking up. "Do you know him very well?"

Flavio waved dismissively. "He's just a client. He seems docile."

"I've actually decided I'm leaving that job."

His eyebrows shot up. "You got a better offer?"

"I'm thinking I should take some time to find the right thing."

After they'd eaten, Huck rose and started to clear the plates.

"Can I help?" Truman said as he handed his over.

Huck chuckled. "Don't be silly."

As he stepped into the kitchen, Flavio leaned back in his chair.

"I like you two," he said. "Maybe we can do some work together. Especially if Truman is soon to be unemployed."

"What kind of work?" Celeste said.

"Well, you've seen the fashion line." He spread his hands. "We also run a cryptocurrency exchange. There's always stuff to do for both. Can either of you run graphics software?"

"I can," Celeste said. "To do what, exactly?"

"You could help sort out a bunch of digital files. Will it mess up your day job?"

"My time at the gallery is pretty flexible."

"Let me get your digits," Flavio said, and pulled out his phone.

As Celeste recited her number, Truman eyed Alicia. Her brow furrowed, and her mouth was a tight line.

Huck returned, and they chatted some more, although Flavio talked the most, and talked louder than anyone else. Eventually Celeste slid her chair back.

"We should go."

Once they'd said their thank-yous, and exchanged good-byes, they went out into the cold night air and walked up the block to Celeste's car. After they'd climbed in, Truman spoke.

"They're certainly a tight little trio."

"A tripod is the most stable social structure," she said, twisting the key in the ignition. "They're a solid tripod."

"When they invite you for dinner, they mean just that. No canapés, no home tour, no messing around."

Celeste laughed as she pulled away from the curb.

"Alicia and Huck both defer to Flavio," Truman said.

"I noticed that."

"Huck was acting like their staff."

"Flavio is definitely the boss," she said. "He talked over Alicia several times, and she just bit her tongue and let him do it."

"Do you think Huck is sleeping with either of the siblings?"

"I don't get that vibe. Huck is definitely into guys—you, specifically, from the way he was drooling when he looked at you."

"I wondered about that," Truman said.

"It was unmistakable. But Flavio seems straight to me."

"Definitely."

Braking for a red light, Celeste looked out the window at the block-long row of tents and clutter and shopping carts piled with tatty possessions.

"When Flavio said 'Let's do some work,' I'm thinking he means work for him, not with him," Truman said.

"That's my sense of it too. I figured we might gain some insight into how they got hold of Yaz's work."

"Thanks for volunteering to do it."

"Yaz is my friend. And you can pay me for being your operative when she pays you."

"At this point I'm thinking we'll just split the fee down the middle."

As she pulled up at Truman's building, Celeste eyed the little clock on the dash. "You know, it's not that late. I wonder if we shouldn't be out drinking somewhere?"

"I'm kind of wiped out," Truman said. "Besides, Friday night is amateur night. Lawyers and accountants and office drones."

"Good point."

Before he climbed out, he leaned in for an air kiss.

ELEVEN

ON SATURDAY MORNING CELESTE got settled at the gallery, and put some mellow house music on the sound system. The place was quiet, as it usually was, and she enjoyed the solitude until sometime after lunch, when Saffron came in, and chatted for a while, then went upstairs to her desk. No one had scheduled a visit, but a couple of weekend walk-ins came in from the street and did a circuit of the gallery.

Celeste's cell phone rang, and when she checked, she saw that it was Flavio.

"Hey, beautiful," he said when she picked up. "Do you want to go to Santa Barbara? I'm making a day trip. I need to talk to a client."

"That's actually tempting," she said. "There's a gallery up there I've been wanting to check out."

"So let's go. Be spontaneous. If we leave soon,

we'll get there in daylight."

She considered her outfit—dark tweed pants and a gray cardigan. That would work for a car trip.

"What the hell," Celeste said finally. "I'm ready whenever."

"Can I pick you up?"

"I'll come to your office."

"You can park in the back, so you won't have to worry about the meters."

Celeste ended the call and went up the blue metal stairs. When she stood in the doorway to the little office, Saffron leaned back in her chair and swiveled to face her.

"Darling."

Saffron was dressed down today, by her standards, in designer jeans and a print blouse, her hair piled in a casual beehive. It didn't matter what she wore; with her annoyingly thin frame, everything looked good on her.

"I'm going to Santa Barbara for the afternoon," Celeste said. "I'll check out some of the galleries."

"Ooh, great idea. There's money in that town. It'll be good to know what those people are buying. Are there any appointments this afternoon that I'll need to handle?"

"Nothing's scheduled."

Celeste went back downstairs and grabbed her bag, then walked out to the alley, closing the fire door behind her and locking it. She drove to

Truman's loft and rang the bell.

His voice came through the static on the tinny little speaker: "Who—at?"

"It's me," she said, raising her voice. "Let me in."

As she reached the top of the stairs, Truman pulled open the door.

"Soda or caffeine?" he said when she stepped in.

"Neither—I can't stay for long. I'm going to Santa Barbara with Flavio."

Truman's eyebrows shot up. "Wow—I knew he was being flirty. I guess he's into you."

"Maybe."

"Are you going to sleep with him?"

"I'm not sure if it's worth it. He's kind of a gasbag."

"He's not unhot, though, for a straight guy, and it's a long drive. I'm sure you'll learn more about him."

"Inevitably," Celeste said, and gestured toward the bathroom. "I wanted to make a withdrawal. I'm getting low on cash."

"Of course," he said, and strode over to his clothes rack, and wheeled it out, and grabbed the aluminum stepladder that was propped against the wall. Pulling it open, he set it next to the bathroom wall, then climbed up a few steps.

Several wrenches spanned the gap between the inner and outer walls. They were short enough that the ends couldn't be seen from below, and each had a cord tied to it. Pulling up one of them, hand over hand, Truman produced a dusty canvas bag and tossed it down to her.

Celeste set it on the floor and pulled open the heavy zipper, revealing bundles of cash tied up in elastic bands. She pulled the band off one of the bundles, and counted out a few thousand, then set the bills aside and looked up.

"Do you need any?"

"Get me two grand," he said.

She peeled more notes off, then stretched the elastic around the bundle again, and zipped the bag closed, and handed it to Truman. He climbed back up a step and slid it into the gap, and lowered it again, concealing it inside the wall, and repositioned the wrench.

On his first case, Truman had stumbled into the opportunity to grab all this dough, the proceeds of a drug sale, after the dealers had been popped and before the police had found it. He'd left some of it for the cops to impound, so as far as the dealers knew, the police had all of it. Whatever discrepancy they might have heard about would have been written off. Sometimes it still made his heart pound, the possibility that someone might come looking for it, but as time went on that seemed less and less likely.

"I must say, it's lasting longer than I thought it would," Celeste said, watching him work.

"We're both being pretty frugal."

"My cousin works for an accountant. He said

that when someone gets a cash inheritance or a windfall, they usually spend it within a year."

Truman stepped down and folded the ladder. "It's a lot harder to spend when we can't put it in the bank."

Celeste stashed the cash in her bra, then adjusted her breasts.

"Don't space out and let some frat boy motorboat you," Truman said. "You'll make him rich."

She scoffed. "What are you up to today?"

"If Flavio's out of town, it might be a good time to talk to one of the other legs of the tripod."

Celeste waved as she left. Once he'd locked the door behind her, Truman dug out his phone and called Huck, glad that he picked up.

"So what are you up to?" Truman said.

"I'm working. We don't really take weekends off."

"Can you take some time today? I thought we could hang out."

"I can after six. You want to call me then?"

They must be pretty busy if he couldn't take a few hours off, Truman thought, once he'd ended the call. But then the vibe he got last night wasn't that Huck was working for himself—it felt more like he was working for Flavio.

——◆——

ONCE SHE'D LEFT TRUMAN'S place, Celeste pulled into the alley behind the Eurorapt office. The gate in the black-painted steel fence was rolled open, and she nosed the little car inside, and parked next to a dark-green Jaguar. It wasn't new, with classic lines rather than a modern shape, but she didn't know about cars, and had no idea how old it was.

Flavio stepped out the back door of the building.

"Hey, beautiful," he called to her. "We'll take my wheels."

Once he'd unlocked it, she climbed into the passenger side, and Flavio backed into the alley.

"This is quite the ride," she said, looking over the plush interior and the wood-grain dashboard.

"Thank you," he said, shifting into Park and climbing out again, leaving his door hanging open.

It wasn't actually a compliment, but Celeste didn't need to point that out. She watched as he rolled the gate closed.

"Are you ready?" he said, climbing in behind the wheel.

"Let's roll."

Flavio laughed, his tone deep and rich. This was the positive side of the guy's bluster, she realized, eyeing him sidelong. He was always so upbeat, ready to flash that smile.

He navigated toward the freeway, and soon they were on the 101, cruising through Hollywood. The traffic wasn't bad for a Saturday, and Flavio got in the left lane, driving as fast as the traffic allowed but not weaving around like a maniac. Once they were through the Cahuenga Pass, the road straightened out.

"How lucky am I," Flavio said, "to spend the day with a beautiful woman?"

"You keep using that word. I get the feeling it's one of your favorites."

"It doesn't mean it's not true."

"I'm not complaining. I'm happy to be considered attractive."

"Are you serious?" he demanded, glancing at her. "You're gorgeous."

"So what's this cryptocurrency business you talked about?"

"Did I mention that?"

"Maybe it was your sister."

"Well, when you acquire crypto, it has to be kept somewhere. Why not with me?"

"So you're like a banker?"

"It's called an exchange. The idea is that people can buy and sell through the exchange. Like a stock exchange."

"And you get a cut of each transaction."

He smiled. "Very good. You could be in finance."

Crypto had much less to do with the finance industry than it did with tech-industry stans and libertarians, she knew, looking out the window at the city flashing by. The kind of people who wanted quick profits or to hide their activities from the tax collector.

Flavio clicked on the radio, and they listened

to pop music, and gazed at the endless Pacific when it appeared along the highway. The low winter sun was already dropping toward the water.

The traffic slowed near Santa Barbara, but not for long, and Flavio exited into the town.

"Where is your gallery?" he said, braking for a stoplight.

Celeste pulled out her phone and checked. "It's right around the corner from the art museum."

"I know where that is."

A minute later he pulled up at a corner on State Street.

"Call me," he said, watching her climb out.

"Or vice versa."

"I'm not sure how long I'll be."

"It doesn't matter," Celeste said. "I'll wander around the other galleries."

"There you go." Once she'd closed the door, he pulled back into the traffic.

Celeste walked down the side street to the gallery and found the entrance. A sign in the glass said BACK AT 5 P.M. She checked the time; it was just after four. At least the place wasn't closed for the day. She could entertain herself for that long.

Back on State Street she stopped into some clothing stores. This was definitely an upscale town, she realized, after checking price tags in a few of the boutiques. Around five, when daylight was fading to twilight, she walked back to the gallery. The sign was gone. Pulling the door open, she found a gray-haired guy sitting at a desk behind a service counter. No one else was here. He looked up and greeted her as she stepped inside.

Celeste acknowledged him and then stepped over to look at the paintings on the wall across from his desk. It was disappointing—she knew what this stuff was. A subset of surrealism done with organic forms and muted colors, it had been around for a while. One reviewer had called it "thrashed surrealism." She'd been hoping for something she hadn't already seen, some innovation, or at least a more informative collection.

"Who curated this show?" she called to the man at the desk.

"I did." He pulled off his glasses as he looked up. "This is my gallery. Are you a buyer?"

"I do what you do," she said, stepping toward him.

"Are you familiar with the genre?"

"Can you tell me what you know about it?"

He stood up, and came around the counter, and talked about the paintings, gesturing to them and leading her close to a couple to narrate the details. Most of the artists were from LA, and she didn't learn anything new, but it was interesting at least to hear the work described in his words. A competent salesman, he name-dropped the twentieth-century artists who had nothing to do with this work, beyond perhaps a hint of inspiration for these modern creators, adding value by cognitive association alone.

"Let me know if you have any specific questions," he said finally, and went back to his desk.

Celeste wandered toward the back of the gallery, studying the pieces, wondering how quickly they moved. The sound of the front door opening came, but she didn't bother to look, as she was around the corner, out of view of the entrance. She registered two men in conversation, but tuned them out, until she recognized the voice of the newcomer—Flavio. She walked back toward the front desk.

"Cryptocurrency is the place to be, my friend," Flavio was saying. He had his palms braced on the counter, leaning toward the gallery owner's desk. "Eventually it's going to run everything."

"Are you sure it's not just a passing fad that'll bottom out in a year or two? Once the early adopters clean out the newcomers?"

Flavio glanced over at Celeste as she approached, but didn't acknowledge her presence. "Crypto is the future. Right now is a great time to get into it because it's only going to increase in value."

"A man who knows the future," the guy said, raising his eyebrows.

"In that respect, I do." Flavio pulled a business card out of his hip pocket and set it on the counter. "I run a crypto exchange. It's like a bank. Don't hesitate to call me—you don't want to miss out."

As he straightened up he winked at Celeste,

and nodded toward the door. Celeste thanked the owner and followed Flavio out to the street. It was dark out now. Flavio put an arm around her waist as they walked.

"You gave him the hard sell," she said.

"People with money are the target clients for the exchange."

"From what I saw in there, I'd guess that he's art-rich and cash-poor."

"Do you want to eat?" Flavio said. "There are dozens of restaurants on the main street."

TWELVE

IT WAS WELL AFTER dark when Huck finally called.

"Do you want to eat?" he said, when Truman picked up. "I know a great sushi place. Can you eat fish?"

"I don't," Truman said, "but if it's a real sushi bar, there'll be plenty of other stuff."

"What does 'real' mean?"

"Run by a sushi chef and not prep cooks."

"This guy is Japanese. His name is Ken."

"That sounds real enough."

"I can pick you up," Huck said.

Truman recited his address. "Phone me when you get here. I'll come down."

FARTHER UP THE STREET Flavio and Celeste

found an Italian place, and sat at a courtyard table under a glowing heat lamp. They ordered food and a bottle of red wine.

Once they'd clinked their wineglasses, Flavio met her gaze. "I had a quick look at the art in that gallery. What makes it good enough to fill a room with it?"

"Good is subjective," Celeste said. "Like with fashion. Just because a reviewer or an influencer is promoting it doesn't mean it's objectively better than something else. All that really matters is whether you like it or not. I ask my clients, 'Can you stand to look at it every day in your living room or your office?'"

"To me it would be good if I could resell it for more than I bought it for."

"That's a different way to value art. As an investment. I get lots of those clients too."

"Don't you think art was better in the Renaissance?" Flavio said, swirling the contents of his wineglass. "Rafael and Caravaggio? Venus on the scallop shell, or God touching Adam's finger? That stuff is stunning."

"Every time I see that painting of Venus it makes me feel like I'm wearing a collar that's too tight."

He laughed, and sat back as the server stepped up with their plates. After they'd taken a few bites, Flavio gestured with his fork.

"Do you know a kind of necklace called a choker?"

"Sure."

"We had a connection with a woman who designed them. I wanted to manufacture them. She said they were going to come back in style, and we'd be able to sell them for a huge markup. But Alicia said you should never wear something named after a violent crime."

Celeste chuckled. "She makes a good point."

"So you don't like Botticelli?" Flavio said. "Adam and God on the ceiling?"

"*The Creation of Adam* is by Michelangelo. Those artists worked within the strictures of the church, right, so their creativity was stifled. Like a choker."

"That gallery up the street felt stifling to me. Everything was so dark. Why don't modern artists paint like Botticelli and Michelangelo?"

Celeste held his gaze. "Because religion doesn't matter anymore, and everything is sex."

Flavio guffawed and sat back. "So that abstract stuff was about sex?"

"It's sexier than freaking Botticelli." She picked up her wineglass and drained it.

"You're such an intriguing woman."

"Thank you. Does that mean you can't really figure me out?"

"It means I want to get to know you better. My client said that his house was available if I wanted to stay over."

"Are you going to?"

"If I do, you'll have to stay as well."

"Not necessarily," Celeste said. "I can take the train back to the city."

He watched her, his gaze intent. "I don't want you to take the train. I want you to stay."

She pursed her lips for a moment. "I don't have a toothbrush or anything."

"My client has supplies."

Celeste sighed. If she stayed, of course she was going to sleep with him.

———◆———

TRUMAN WAS PULLING ON his shoes when Huck texted:

I'm here.

When he got down to the street, he saw Huck sitting in a convertible. It was red with a wood panel running its length. Despite the cool winter evening he had the top down.

"How old is this thing?" Truman said, walking up to it.

Huck grinned at him. "It's an '85. It's called a LeBaron."

"Why would you drive this?"

"Is it not cool?"

"It's pretty impractical. You can't lock anything inside."

"Sometimes beauty is painful, Truman."

He laughed and climbed in. "That's what women say after the fabled Brazilian wax job."

"Is that when they wax their jittles? That does

sound painful."

Huck pulled into the street and drove a few blocks to Little Tokyo. They could have walked, Truman knew, and it would have been faster than the time it took him to find a street space. But at heart most Angelenos with the means were car people.

They climbed out, and Huck left the top down, and led the way to a narrow little sushi bar. The place looked authentic, and they sat at the counter, surveying the menu board. The prices weren't cheap, but they weren't bougie either.

"Do you want to split a beer?" Huck said.

"Sure."

When the chef stepped up, in a clean white jacket and a tight little cap, he greeted Huck as if he were a regular.

"One of those big bottles of beer," he said, and then ordered several plates by their menu number.

"First a *tamago*," Truman said, "and then a couple of *kappa*, and a *kampyo*, if you have it."

"I do," the guy said, and stepped away.

A woman brought the bottle and a couple of glasses, and soon after their first plates arrived.

After he'd sampled the *tamago*, Truman eyed Huck. Despite being recognized as a repeat customer, he was a tyro with the food, eating it with chopsticks.

"So what do you get out of working with Alicia and Flavio?" Truman said.

Huck shrugged. "We're making money. I like the work."

"Do you have your own side projects?"

"Mostly we collaborate. There's a lot of work to do on what we've already got going."

The chef set down a plate of shrimp *nigiri* for Huck and a *kappa* for Truman.

"How was the *tamago*?" he said, eyeing Truman.

"Perfect. You clearly know what you're doing."

"Everything here is good," Huck said.

"A connoisseur always orders *tamago* up front," the chef said. "It's a way to keep me on my toes. I wanted to make sure it met your standards."

As he walked away, Huck eyed Truman. "Did you know that?"

"Sushi was a thing for a while. I got good at it. And I didn't order *tamago* to make him hustle— it's how you assess the quality of the place. I could tell right away he's a five-star chef."

Huck frowned. "Is that why you're eating with your hands? Because you're good at it?"

"Sushi is expensive because fish is expensive, but it's not fancy. It's meant to be simple finger food. Like sandwiches or hot dogs."

"I'll take your word for it."

"So the fashion line and the fabrics keep you busy," Truman said, and reached for his beer glass. "But you've never thought about working for yourself?"

"It's not just fashion," he said, raising his

eyebrows. "Flavio is trying to set up a crypto exchange."

"Doesn't that require coding? Who does that part of it?"

"Flavio seems to be getting it together. He says he knows enough to get things started. The technical details are above my skill level."

Munching his roll, Truman eyes him sidelong. That didn't quite align with Flavio's story. Yesterday he'd said that the exchange was already operating.

The chef set down another plate of *kampyo* for Truman.

"Did you order that?" Huck said.

"I didn't. But it's too tasty to send back." He picked up a piece and bit into it.

"That's not yours."

"It is now," Truman said, with his mouth half full, and picked up another piece.

———•———

After they'd eaten, Celeste and Flavio walked to his car, and he drove into a neighborhood not far from the town center, and pulled into the driveway of a Spanish-style bungalow. They both climbed out, and Flavio studied his phone for a moment, then punched a four-digit code into the keypad lock.

"This looks like a rental," Celeste said, stepping in after him and looking around the front room. The place was furnished, but there was nothing personal, no photos or books or clutter.

"My client uses it as a hospitality unit."

"What kind of business is he in?"

"Something about garbage. Recycling or hauling."

Interesting that he needed a hospitality unit in that business, Celeste thought. Stepping into the bathroom, she found a couple of robes, and towels, and a toothbrush, even moisturizer. Her phone buzzed in her pocket, and she pulled it out to check. It was a text from Truman:

How's SB?

She thumb-typed a brief reply:

I'm staying over.

His response made her smile:

Score.

Walking back into the main room, she found Flavio in the kitchen, pouring wine into a couple of glasses.

"Do you like chianti?" he said.

"Why not?" she said, even though they'd just split a bottle of red, and she could still feel a little buzz from it.

Flavio handed her a glass, and clinked his against it. She actually didn't like the stuff, she realized, once she'd taken a sip. It was too sharp.

"You're so beautiful," Flavio said, holding her gaze.

"I blame my parents."

He chuckled, and set his glass down, and moved closer. Leaning in, Celeste met his mouth, and spent a minute in it, the warmth, and the firmness, and the acrid taste of the chianti.

"Come on," she said, and led the way to the bedroom.

"You're a take-charge woman."

She laughed. "You can't tell me this isn't what you were thinking of."

"It's exactly what I was thinking of."

A minute later they were undressed and on the bed. Unlike in his business persona, Flavio took his time, exploring her body with his hands. Once he was hard, Celeste climbed up to straddle him. Flavio seemed content not to be in charge.

———◆———

WHEN THEY STEPPED OUT of the sushi bar, Truman paused on the sidewalk, and shoved his hands in his pockets against the cold.

"Do you want to walk around the neighborhood, or maybe go back to my place?"

"Option B," Huck said. "Definitely."

Truman chuckled, and they walked back to Huck's car, and drove to Truman's building. Huck nosed into a street space out front, then spent a minute putting the top up.

"Will Redge be safe here?" Huck said.

"Is that your car's name?"

"It's short for Reginald." He frowned. "Doesn't

your car have a name?"

"I don't have a car," Truman said. "Redge will be fine if we contract with one of my neighborhood service providers." He stepped toward the alley beside the building, and the long row of tents, and cupped his hands around his mouth. "Beretta," he called.

A minute later Beretta appeared, his bulky coat zipped up to his chin. His eyes were bright and he wore a wry grin. Maybe he'd been drinking, or scored some meth.

"Hey, Sunshine," he said. "You need something?"

"Can you watch my friend's car?" Truman said. "I don't want anyone to mess with it."

"Of course. For a small gratuity of twenty dollars, it'll be safe for the night."

"How about a fin?" Truman dug out his wad of cash.

Beretta looked at Huck and gave him the once-over. "He doesn't look like he'll keep you busy for very long. Give me a sawbuck."

Truman peeled a five off his wad and handed it over.

"Thanks, neighbor," Beretta said, and walked back into the alley.

As Truman twisted his key in the front door, Huck spoke in a low voice. "Do you always pay him not to steal cars?"

"He wouldn't do that. But he will keep an eye out. If you think about it, it's cheaper than parking in a paid lot."

Once they'd stepped into the loft, Huck looked around. "This place is huge."

"I have a commercial lease, so I can do whatever I want."

"Did you build that cube?"

"With some help from Celeste's dad. He came to see the place and said it was way too weird to have the plumbing in the middle of the room."

Huck stepped over and looked into the bathroom. "Why was it in the middle of the room?"

"I don't think it always was. The last tenant took the walls with them."

"I get it." He turned to face Truman. "You don't want the head in view of your house guests."

"Were you in the Navy?"

Huck frowned. "Why do you say that?"

"You called it 'the head.' You sound like a sailor."

"I was never in the service."

Truman stepped closer, and put his hands on Huck's waist, and leaned into his mouth, warm and taut and intent. Huck pulled him toward the bed and deftly unbuckled his belt, and pulled Truman's shirt off.

Once he had his own clothes off, he pushed Truman onto the bed and straddled him, mouthing Truman's neck and ear.

"I want to fuck you," he said softly.

"Yeah," Truman said, and grinned, and reached

for a condom in the bedside table.

Huck was hard enough, and soon penetrated him, working up to pounding him.

Once they'd both climaxed, Truman stretched out, panting to catch his breath.

"That was hot," he said.

Huck chuckled and got up, and went to the bathroom, returning briefly to throw Truman a towel. A minute later he heard the shower go on.

Truman dozed until Huck got back, then shifted onto his side and put an arm around his chest.

"Is Huck short for anything?"

"No, but my whole life I've been called Huckleberry. My mother was a little shortsighted on that one."

"I like your name. It's unique."

"I guess I didn't dislike it enough to change it."

"Was school rough for you?"

"Not too bad, apart from the name harassment. I grew up in an extremely white place, so I was always an outsider."

"Where was that?"

"Utah," Huck said.

"I guess that's about as white as it gets."

"My peers decided I had three parents: a black one, a Latin one, and a Jewish one."

Truman laughed. "I didn't have that problem, but in middle school I definitely learned to run."

"Why is that?"

"Some of the athletic types used to chase me around at lunchtime."

"What did they do to you when they caught you?"

"I never let that happen."

THIRTEEN

WHEN CELESTE WOKE IT took a minute to remember where she was. This bed was comfortable, and daylight streamed in through the sheers. She could smell toast. Eventually it came to her, and she went into the bathroom, and pulled on a robe, and walked out to the kitchen.

"It's just basic continental," Flavio said, looking up from the counter, where he was buttering the toast.

"I'm grateful to get anything. Thanks for doing it."

"Sit down," he said, and nodded toward the table.

There was a mug of coffee here already, and she took a satisfying sip. Flavio had put out a box of corn flakes, and she poured some into a bowl, and then oat milk, and stirred it around before she took a bite. Flavio dropped into the chair across from her, a grin on his face.

Celeste waved her spoon. "What?"

"You have such a look on your face. Like you're experiencing that cereal very deeply."

"Do you know how crunchy these things are? It's like week-old tortilla chips. I'm worried about my teeth."

"You don't usually eat cereal?"

"Not this stuff. It's a little weird."

Flavio chuckled. "Oh, Celeste, I like you. You make me laugh."

———◆———

WHEN TRUMAN WOKE, HE turned over, and saw Huck across the room, naked and peering into the refrigerator.

"What are you looking for?" he called to him.

Huck swung the door closed. "You have no food here."

"I eat out a lot."

"Do you want to go get breakfast?"

"Let me wash up," Truman said, and rolled out of bed.

When they got down to the street, Huck nodded to his car.

"Your friend kept his word. I'm kind of surprised it's still here."

"We'll go that way," Truman said, gesturing up the block. "There's usually a *lonchera* or two on

142

the side street."

"What's that?"

"A lunch wagon."

"Is that like a food truck?"

"Food trucks sell twenty-dollar hamburgers and eight-dollar gourmet doughnuts," Truman said. "A *lonchera* is for working people."

"Do you speak Spanish?"

"Enough to get fed."

They found a truck, and ordered burritos, and ate them standing nearby on the sidewalk.

"This is good," Huck said, holding it well away from his body, as if he were fearful of the sauce dripping on his shirt.

"It's definitely better than what I could have made."

"And a lot cheaper than hipster hot dogs."

Walking back toward Truman's loft, Huck briefly squeezed him around the shoulder. "I have an errand to do today. Do you want to come with?"

"Where's your errand?"

"It's not far. It won't take long."

Truman eyed him sidelong. Flavio had said they needed help. Maybe Huck was auditioning him for their crew.

———◆———

AFTER THEY CLEARED OUT of the borrowed house, Flavio navigated the Jaguar onto the 101, driving fast in the southbound lanes. Celeste sent Saffron a text to tell her when she'd be in, even though Saffron didn't care whether the gallery was open or not. These days Celeste earned mostly from commissions rather than an hourly wage, and people with the resources to spend big considered their time valuable, so they called ahead to arrange to visit the gallery. Still, it was Sunday, with more foot traffic in the Arts District, so Celeste felt like the place should be open for the walk-ins.

She tucked her phone away and gazed out at the ocean, bright blue in the morning sun.

"What are you thinking about?" Flavio said, glancing over at her.

"The ancient Greeks had different words for different ways the ocean looked," she said. "Something like bright blue and dark blue, but not really about the color. I read that it's hard to translate into modern languages."

"What would they call the way it looks today?"

"I have no idea what the actual words are. I suspect the nuances have been lost to time."

"You're such a romantic."

"It's more about history," she said, meeting his gaze. "Knowing how they saw things illuminates how they thought about the world."

"The Greeks are very good sailors. I was on a ferry in Greece a few years ago. Hundreds of people crossing the water at high speed with no land in sight. All the sailors acted like it was no big deal."

"They've been doing it for a while."

Flavio's phone rang, with the first few bars of a brass-heavy Latin tune. He fished it out and held it to his ear.

"How are you, my friend," he shouted, and then listened. "Of course I can transfer the funds, but I think you're making a mistake … It doesn't happen instantly … Of course the exchange is liquid. But there's an interface between the dollar and the new currencies, you know? It takes a minute or two to sort it out … It'll happen. Just give me a few days. It's the weekend …" His tone rose. "I'm telling you, you have to play it cool," he said, and then ended the call. Tucking his phone away, he muttered, "Idiot."

"Business trouble?" Celeste said.

"So few people have true vision. They get stuck in a rut."

She looked out the window, gazing at the sea, and decided not to ask a follow-up. Azure, maybe, that specific shade of blue. Not as dark as indigo. She tried to intuit the way the Greeks had thought of it, the quality of light and dark in the water rather than the hue.

Flavio interrupted her thoughts. "So we talked about you working with Eurorapt. Can you come in and look at some stuff tomorrow?"

"Why not?" she said, turning toward him. "I'll come over in the morning."

"It's not going to be a conflict at the gallery?"

"I basically set my own hours there."

Once they were back in the city, and drove

through the Cahuenga Pass, Flavio pulled up behind the Eurorapt office and rolled the gate open, then parked in the little yard.

Celeste climbed out, and stretched, then unlocked her car. Flavio stood on the other side of the Jag, watching her, his gaze intent.

"What?" she said.

"You're not going to say good-bye?"

Suppressing a grin, she stepped around and put her hands on his neck, and planted him with an intense open kiss, lingering in it for a moment.

She pulled back and raised her eyebrows. "Better?"

He took a breath. "Much, much better."

Celeste walked back to her car and pulled open the driver's door.

"See you tomorrow, yeah?" Flavio called to her.

She chuckled and climbed in. As she backed out of the little yard, he was still watching her. It felt a little intense, a little weird, like maybe he was really into her. But that didn't quite make sense— they hadn't spent that much time together.

Home first, she decided, before she went to the gallery. It wouldn't be too bad to go to work in these clothes, but she wanted to change, and navigated toward the Sixth Street Bridge.

———◆———

IN FRONT OF TRUMAN'S place, Huck unlocked his car, and they both climbed in. He twisted the key in the ignition.

"I'm amazed," Huck said. "The engine is still here."

"Beretta said it would be safe, so it was safe," Truman said, and pulled on his seat belt.

Huck navigated onto the westbound 10, the road noise making conversation impossible in the ragtop car. He exited onto Crenshaw and headed north, and soon they were in Hancock Park, an old-money neighborhood. On a long block of mansions, set well back from the street and fronted by verdant manicured lawns, Huck slowed and then turned into a driveway.

There was a for-sale sign in the yard, Truman saw. Huck pulled all the way up the drive, next to the house.

"Whose place is this?" Truman said.

"A friend's."

Huck climbed out of the car and walked to the side door. Truman followed and watched as he crouched at the black real-estate lockbox that hung from the door handle. He knew the code, quickly punching it in and then pulling the box open to grab the key.

Twisting it in the deadbolt, he stepped inside, and focused on the alarm panel, silencing its strident beeping. He knew the code for that as well, but Truman wasn't able to see the numbers, as Huck stood close to the panel, shielding it with his body.

They were in the kitchen, and the place looked lived in, with countertop appliances, food canisters, a little round table and chairs.

"Nice place," Truman said, walking over to the hallway and looking into the sprawling front room. "How do you know this guy?"

"I actually slept with him." Huck stepped away from the alarm. "I need to get some data from his computer."

Truman followed him into a hallway and then into a little office that looked out on the grassy backyard. Huck sat at the desk and grabbed the mouse, peering at the computer screen.

"Does he know you're here?" Truman said.

"It's fine. He's in New York for the shows."

"He must trust you, if he gave you the codes for the key box and for the alarm."

Huck chuckled. "There's no security cameras, and he's not the kind of guy who could get the alarm system to tell him if or when it was turned off. He'll never know I was here."

That wasn't the same as having permission to be here, Truman thought, feeling his heart start to pound. Why had he followed Huck in here? At least he hadn't touched anything yet, so he hadn't left his fingerprints.

Huck glanced at his phone, then typed on the computer's keyboard. That meant it was locked, and he'd made a note of the password.

"You have access to his computer," Truman said. "What are you doing, exactly?"

Not looking up, Huck didn't respond, his fingers moving fast on the keys, his focus intent.

Truman wandered over to the window adjacent to the desk, and glanced out at the yard, then turned to squint at the computer screen, trying to parse what Huck was up to.

It was definitely about copying files. Truman could see he was dragging things into a cloud drive. It was graphics, he realized—the file icons were for tiff images and vectors.

"Damn it," Huck muttered.

"What's wrong?"

"Some of what I wanted isn't here. You'd think in this day and age people would just use cloud storage."

"Do you want to call this guy and ask him about it?"

"I can't do that."

If Huck was aware that Truman was watching him work, he didn't seem concerned. What he did next was telling—he pulled up the quick-access list of logins and deleted one of them, the cloud account he'd just been using. Next he opened the browser history and deleted the last few entries. Truman knew what that meant. He didn't want to leave tracks.

With a keystroke Huck locked the computer, then stood up.

"Let's vamoose."

"I shouldn't have come in with you," Truman said. "I've shed DNA all over the place."

Huck scoffed. "No one's going to be checking for that. I didn't do anything wrong."

"So what did you do?" Truman demanded.

"Come on—we should go."

Huck strode through the house, back to the kitchen door, and reset the alarm. Once he'd herded Truman outside he locked up again, replacing the key in the lockbox.

They climbed into Huck's convertible, and as he backed down the driveway, Truman memorized the house number, and when they reached the corner, he made a mental note of the name of the street.

"I need to get to the office," Huck said. "Can I drop you at your place?"

"Did we just burgle someone's house?" Truman demanded.

"I know the guy. I've been helping him with computer stuff."

Again that wasn't a straight answer, Truman thought, eyeing him sidelong. Last night Huck had said he wasn't very computer savvy, and copying graphics files didn't feel like tech support. Biff Sturgis would say those contradictions meant the story was bunco.

When they got back downtown, Huck pulled up in front of his building, then leaned over to meet his mouth for a moment before Truman climbed out.

"Bye, hot stuff," he said, and pulled into the street.

When he got up to his loft, Truman sat at his desk, and pulled open his laptop, and searched for the address of that house. He didn't even have to dig into the real estate sales records. The result at the top of the list said "Record Price for Hancock Park Tudor Revival." It was an article on a real estate blog, dated a few years ago, and when he clicked on it, the accompanying photo was definitely the house they'd just been in. The purchaser was named as Neil Nephard. Why did that name sound familiar?

When he searched for it, he found that Neil Nephard was a designer—a big name in activewear, mostly for men. He did men's and women's swimsuits, and men's underpants, and his signature product, a trendy line of board shorts. He scrolled through several pages of product images. Truman had definitely seen these clothes before.

He found a portrait of Neil on his company's website. The guy looked to be in his sixties, and was a little chubby, or maybe had that aging muscle thing going on. Either this was an old photo or frosted tips were back in vogue. Despite the hair, Neil had a swarthy look, maybe with some Asian or Native American heritage.

Truman sat back and took a breath. Huck had the lockbox code to this guy's house. Was that the same as having the key? Maybe it meant they hadn't technically burgled the house. But did Huck really have a right to go in there? More significantly, why would this trendy designer let Huck dig around on his computer?

FOURTEEN

AT THE GALLERY, CELESTE was settled in at the desk near the entrance, wading through the office email, when the front door swung open. The place had been empty since she'd arrived, although Saffron said there had been some weekend walk-ins earlier in the day.

Celeste sat back in her chair when she saw the newcomer—it was Alicia, wearing a black blazer and an orangey-pink floral skirt. She had an intent look on her face.

"What are you doing here?" Celeste said.

Alicia scowled. "I see you've had time to fix your lipstick."

"What are you talking about?"

"I know what you did with Flavio. He had that shade all over his face when he came into the office, so I watched the security footage for the back door. I saw exactly how it happened."

"You seem very protective of your brother."

"We tell people that we're siblings, but that's just for business." Alicia waved an arm and raised her voice. "He's with me."

Celeste took a deep breath and spoke as calmly as she could. "How was I supposed to know that? He never said anything about it. You should be pissed at Flavio. Not me."

At the sound of heels clanking on the blue metal staircase, they both looked over to see Saffron descending. She was wearing high-waisted dark-brown trousers and a print blouse, her hair styled back around her ears.

"Please tell me you're not arguing over a man," Saffron said.

"Alicia, this is Saffron Swati," Celeste said. "She's the owner of the gallery."

"Is that blouse Loudermilk?" Alicia said.

Saffron raised her eyebrows. "You have a good eye."

"I recognize the fabric, not the cut. Is it from this season?"

"It's couture, darling."

"Well, on you, it looks flawless."

Saffron looked to Celeste. "I like her. She can stay."

"I have to go to that show," Celeste said, and sat up. "Are you coming with?"

Saffron shook her head. "That bus-bench

lawyer is coming in soon."

"I forgot." Celeste rose. "Upsell him on Martina's pieces. Those guys always go for that stuff. Tell him it's investment-grade."

"Good idea."

Alicia waved an arm. "We're not done here."

"So come with me," Celeste said. "We can talk on the way. You're interested in art, aren't you?"

"Are you messing with me?" she demanded.

Celeste held her gaze for a moment. "No."

Her eyes narrowed, calculating. Finally she threw up her hands. "Lead on."

Celeste strode toward the back door, and locked it once Alicia had stepped into the alley. She climbed into her little blue car and reached across to unlock the passenger door.

"How come your alley is so clean and free of tents?" Alicia said, once she'd climbed in. "There's no graffiti either."

"The business owners got together and hired security to keep them out." Celeste backed into the alley and headed toward the street. "There's usually a guard floating around."

"It's starting to feel like the way things work in developing countries. Instead of public services, you have to pay for everything yourself."

"If we didn't pay for private security, you know this would be a tent encampment," Celeste said. "Preventing that is a lot easier than trying to dislodge them later."

They drove in silence for a while, Alicia sitting

with her arms folded, gazing out the side window. Celeste accelerated up the ramp onto the freeway. She knew she didn't have to say anything. Alicia would get into it soon enough. When she finally spoke, she sounded calmer.

"What are your intentions with Flavio?" she said. "Are you into him?"

"I'm not. I thought it was just a fling." She glanced over to meet her gaze. "With a single guy."

"He's not single."

She didn't respond to that, and Alicia was quiet again, until Celeste exited onto surface streets.

"So where are we going?"

"East LA College. It's not far."

Once she'd parked in a structure on the campus, Celeste led the way toward the exhibition hall.

"You seem to know your way around," Alicia said, walking abreast.

"I did some classes here."

When they found the exhibition, it was more extensive than Celeste had expected, with several long aisles of paintings and sculptures and installation pieces stretching into the distance. It was the first day, so there were a lot of people here, the families of the student artists, chatting and boisterous and happy.

Alicia glanced around. "It's student art?"

"That's right."

"There's so much of it."

"It hasn't been curated," Celeste said. "In a gallery that's not a good thing, but young people are fresh, and raw, and experimental. You never know what they're going to come up with."

They walked up one of the aisles, gazing at pieces on both sides.

"So you're here to acquire art?" Alicia said.

"Not really. It's more about trying to spot emerging trends. This college is heavily Latin, and Latin Los Angeles is a cultural crucible."

"How do you do that?" she said. "Spot trends, I mean."

"Well, an example is the bright colors." She paused and pointed to a couple of canvases. "I'm already seeing that among professional artists."

"So it's an established trend."

"I think so. These students might not even know that, or care, but it's in the zeitgeist. Something about striving toward optimism."

They walked to the end of the hall and then back in the next aisle.

"So much of it is abstract," Alicia said. "Is that a trend?"

"I'd say that's a long-term arc."

Celeste paused to study a trio of canvases. They'd been done as a set, in earthy colors and horizontal blocky shapes. She could feel the emotion the artist had put into it.

A college-age guy was standing nearby, watching her now as she studied the work. With him was a woman with short hair, older but with the same broad nose.

"Are these yours?" Celeste said.

"They are." His brow furrowed as he stepped closer.

"Can I give you my card?" She fished in her bag and found one, then handed it to him. "I work in a gallery. Maybe you can swing by and show me your portfolio."

"I don't really have a lot of stuff."

"So you'll show me what you do have."

"Are you a buyer?"

"I'm more like an agent." Celeste glanced toward the woman, who stood watching them intently. "I know you're with your family today. Give me a call one day when you're not busy."

He smiled and gestured with the card. "Thanks."

"I can feel the youthful energy thing," Alicia said, strolling with her farther up the aisle. "All the experimentation. Are these artists any good? Like that kid?"

"I'm pretty sure I could sell the hell out of his paintings."

They walked into the next aisle, Celeste pausing occasionally to assess an artwork.

"How do you make money on this?" Alicia said, waving at the space. "Not personally. I mean, in your industry."

"Well, you can open a gallery, and form relationships with artists like this."

"That sounds involved. And capital-intensive."

"You could also rep artists without a gallery, and market their work to galleries or directly to buyers," Celeste said. "You need to have lots of contacts, though."

"That sounds like a sales job. Like with fashion."

"It's probably similar, but the margins are a lot higher." They were back near the entrance, and Celeste took a last look around. "I think I'm done."

Walking back toward the parking structure, Alicia said, "You're not who I thought you were."

Celeste grinned. "A glib hoochie man-stealer?"

"Not that. Just … you're not a crook."

"I can't apologize for getting with Flavio. I didn't know you were together. I wouldn't have done it if I'd known."

Alicia huffed, then said quietly, "I know."

———◆———

AFTER SHE'D DROPPED ALICIA at Eurorapt, Celeste drove to Truman's loft, and parked out front. It felt colder as she climbed out of the car, with the sun gone as twilight set in. When she got upstairs Truman pulled the door open.

"Do you want to make me an espresso?" she said.

"Of course." He stepped over to fire up the machine. "So how was Santa Barbara? Where did you stay?"

Celeste went over to the sofas, and kicked her shoes off, then sprawled on the purple one.

"Flavio's business associate had a guest house."

"I'm thinking somebody got some action," Truman called to her, raising his voice over the sound of the machine. "Is he stacked?"

"Less so than you might think. What's more interesting is that Alicia and Flavio are sleeping together."

"What?" he demanded, carrying two demitasse cups over. "I thought they were brother and sister."

Celeste sat up and took a cup. "She came to the gallery to confront me. Apparently they just tell people they're siblings for business purposes."

"What possible difference could it make in business?" Truman said, dropping onto the adjacent sofa and sipping at his steaming cup.

"I was thinking about that. Maybe it's about agility. If they tell people they're both single, they can use flirting as an unrestricted business tool."

"That actually makes sense. Was she pissed?"

"Totally," Celeste said, and told him about their conversation, and the trip to the student art show.

"It's kind of a dick move of him not to tell you he was involved," Truman said. "Especially when it's with someone you know."

"I think it's a symptom of an oversize ego. It makes me wonder how solid his crypto exchange is."

"Flavio implied that it was already operating, but when Huck talked about it, he spun it differently. Like it was still in development. Biff Sturgis says that kind of contradiction is a telltale sign of bunco."

Celeste chuckled. "I watched Flavio put the crypto hard sell on the owner of the gallery I visited. He made it sound like he was J. P. Morgan. Then on the drive back from Santa Barbara I heard his side of a phone call."

As she related the details, Truman absorbed it all, sipping his espresso.

"It sounds like there might be some hiccups in his crypto exchange," he said finally. "So I had an interesting morning with Huck."

"He slept over?" she said, raising her eyebrows. "I bet he was bossy in bed. That kind of guy always is."

"Not bossy so much as assertive, I'd say. When he's away from Flavio, he's kind of a different guy." He told her about going into Neil Nephard's house.

"I know that designer," Celeste said. "I see that name all the time. He must be raking it in."

"He definitely has a big old house. Huck says he knows him, but to me it felt like Huck was robbing the guy. He made a point of erasing his tracks on that computer."

Celeste sipped her espresso. "I wonder if you should talk to Neil, and find out what's going on? You might be able to figure out how well he knows Huck."

"Good idea." He set his cup down and watched her for a moment. "These people are up to something, aren't they? I can just feel it."

She nodded. "Big time."

Truman took a breath. "Have you eaten?"

"Let's go," she said, and drained her little cup, and rose.

They drove to a taqueria they both liked, north of the freeway in the swath of grubby industrial businesses that stood just outside the Arts District.

After they'd eaten, Truman said, "You know what's fun on Sunday? That place by the market."

"That place is fun. We can dance and blow off some steam."

"Do you need to change?"

"For that place, I'm already dressed up."

She drove to Fourth Street and found an open meter, and they walked up the block to the raucous dance bar. It wasn't that late, but the place seemed busy. The crowd was mixed, men and women and straight and gay, and it always felt accessible, as no one was too worried about their clothes or their hair.

There was no room to sit at the bar, but Celeste leaned in and ordered a gin and tonic and a margarita, stepping back a minute later to hand the lowball to Truman. He led the way into the back, where the dance floor was, and they stood at the edge of it to drink, watching the crowd.

Celeste leaned close and shouted to be heard over the music. "There's tons of guys here."

Truman nodded. "Tons."

The music was good, and once they'd finished the round, they pushed onto the dance floor and let loose. Celeste could feel the sweat in her hair, and for fun bumped hips with a couple of guys, briefly exchanging a howl or a smile. Once she was worn out, she nodded toward the front of the bar, and she and Truman squeezed through the crowd.

Walking back to her car, Celeste hugged him around the waist. "Can I drop you at home?"

"I feel like I should walk," Truman said. "It'll help me cool off."

At the car they exchanged an air-kiss goodbye, and Truman headed toward his own neighborhood. On a long block at the edge of Skid Row he detoured around a long row of sidewalk tents, eventually crossing the street when the encampment spanned the full width from the wall to the gutter. Across the street someone shouted something unintelligible, and he cast a wary eye toward the source, but it wasn't directed at him.

One margarita hadn't really given him a buzz, what with all that dancing, but the cool night air felt good in his hair and on his sweaty shirt.

FIFTEEN

IN THE MORNING CELESTE dressed in a blazer and a wool skirt, checking her look in the floor mirror. She could wear this to the gallery later if she decided to go. In the kitchen she found María, dressed for work, with her hair up, wearing a dark vest with a name tag on it. She was slicing an avocado with a paring knife and arranging it on a slice of toast.

"Do you want some of this?" she said, eyeing Celeste as she walked in.

"That would be great."

Celeste poured a coffee, and sat at the kitchen table, and took a bite of the toast when María set down a plate. She'd scattered some minced poblano on top.

"These avocados are amazing."

"Your father got them from somebody's

backyard tree."

"Those are always the best ones."

María brought her own plate to the table and took the chair across from her. "So where were you on Saturday night?"

"You got my text. I went to Santa Barbara, and stayed over with a friend."

"Not Truman? What kind of friend?"

"It's not what you're thinking," Celeste said, and frowned.

"I'm thinking Saturday night is date night. It must have been a man."

"I went on business."

"Well, if he's nice, I want to meet him," she said, and bit into her toast.

María left before she did, not returning to ask her to move her car. Ernesto was usually the first out in the morning, and he repositioned their vehicles in the driveway when he left. Today he'd guessed right: Celeste would be the last to leave.

Eventually climbing into her car, Celeste backed out of the driveway, and drove to Euro-rapt, and turned into the alley. The gate on the little yard was open, so she pulled in and parked beside the Jag.

Steeling herself with a deep breath, she went to the back door, and eyed the camera above it, pointed down at the fenced-in space. Why hadn't she noticed that? She pounded on the heavy door with the heel of her fist. If Flavio was going to act weird, that was on him, she reminded herself.

Hopefully he and Alicia had worked out their stuff.

A moment later Flavio pushed it open, and greeted her with his usual bluster, and waved her inside. The back room was one big space, with an airy high ceiling and utilitarian fluorescent fixtures dangling below it. Three desks with computers on them sat along one side, and in the middle was a long worktable, not being used for pattern-making or cutting right now, instead piled with bolts of fabric, paperwork, and carefully draped garments, including the tops and dresses from the show the other night. The one made with Yaz's fabric wasn't visible among them.

Alicia was parked at one of the desks, and they exchanged a perfunctory greeting before she looked back to her screen.

"You haven't been here before," Flavio said. "Come through and check out the public space."

He led the way through a door into the room that faced the street. Huck was at one of the desks, and looked up from his screen to say hello.

"I see what you were going for," Celeste said, taking it in.

"Do you?" Flavio said, hands on his hips. "What do you see?"

"Well, it's kind of space-age mixed with industrial chic."

He laughed, his tone deep. "That works." He gestured to a set of sleek lounge chairs. "These used to be in an airline lounge at the airport."

"They definitely have that vibe. So this is where you meet clients?"

"That's the idea." He gestured to the back room. "Come on—I'll get you set up."

Closing the door behind him, Flavio went to the desk next to Alicia's and pulled out the chair.

"This is mine," he said. "Have a seat."

"So what is it that I'm doing today?" Celeste said, dropping into the chair.

"We need to process some images for clothing patterns."

She scooted closer to the monitor. "What kind of software have you got?"

"All the design stuff you'll need." Flavio pointed to the icons on the desktop, then leaned in and grabbed the mouse, and clicked on a folder. "It's these files."

When he clicked on one of them, a line drawing came up. It was the outline of a pant leg, Celeste realized. This was a scan of a pattern.

"You just need to trim off all the text," Flavio said. "Not the measurement numbers, but the corporate stuff. After that we'll print them on manila cardstock on a large-format printer. I don't want someone else's logo on them."

"So it's just about removing text and logos?" Celeste said.

"Right. But make it look like there was nothing there in the first place." He clicked open another file. "Some of these have watermarks. Can you remove those?"

"It might be possible, depending on how they were applied."

"It's all patterns. Line drawings, like this one."

"I already know the software, so I'd say it shouldn't be too difficult."

"Alicia can help you if you have any questions," he said. "I have a meeting."

Ignoring Alicia, he strode to the back door and grabbed a jacket off the coat rack, then stepped outside, slamming the door behind him.

Celeste eyed Alicia. "He seems fine."

She looked up briefly and met her gaze. "Of course he is," she said flatly.

As she opened each of the files, Celeste found that they were all patterns, but like the clothes in the show the other night, they seemed to be a random assemblage—tops and pants and skirts in different styles. All of them were clearly branded with logos and watermarks from several different companies.

She stared at the screen, thinking it through. In fashion it was expected that designers borrowed each other's ideas, but it was definitely not OK to hijack someone else's patterns. Like Yaz's fabric, all this stuff was someone else's intellectual property. If Eurorapt had licensed these files, or had permission to use them, they wouldn't need to scrubbed—this felt like straight-up piracy.

She glanced sidelong at Alicia, sitting there absorbed in her screen, clacking at the keyboard. Was Celeste really going to do this?

—•—

TRUMAN WAS AT THE kitchen counter, starting on his second coffee, when his phone rang. Pulling it out, he saw that it was Flavio.

"Can you give me a hand today?" Flavio said when he picked up. "I need help with some work."

"I thought Celeste was working with you today," Truman said. "If you need me too, I can come to your office later."

"Are you ready now? I'll pick you up. Wear jeans," he said, and ended the call.

Huck must have told him where he lived, Truman realized. Flavio hadn't even asked. The jeans thing felt suspicious, but he went over to his clothes rack and changed into an old pair that he wore for cleaning and painting and helping people move.

He'd barely finished his java when he got a text from Flavio:

I'm downstairs.

When Truman got down to the street, a big box truck was stopped in front of the building, blocking his view of the street, its heavy diesel engine idling. He paused and looked around for a car—Celeste had said Flavio drove a green Jag.

The passenger door of the cargo truck swung open, and Flavio's voice came from inside the cab: "Truman."

He walked over and stepped on the running board to look inside. Flavio was behind the wheel, beaming at him.

"I'm almost afraid to ask what you want me to do today," Truman said.

"It's nothing you can't handle. Get in."

Once he'd climbed up and slammed the door, Flavio nosed the behemoth away from the curb and rolled up the street.

"Do you need a special license to drive something this big?" Truman said, raising his voice over the rumble of the engine.

"Probably."

At least people saw it coming, or maybe they heard it. A porter crossing the street with a rack of clothes glanced at the truck and then quickened his pace to hustle out of the way. When Flavio slowed to make a right turn, the pedestrians waiting at the corner eyed the vehicle warily, waiting for him to make the turn even though they had the crossing signal.

"Why do you need a truck this big?"

"I need to move a few things," Flavio said, and waved a hand, focusing on the traffic.

That sounded like an understatement, Truman thought. This rig was built to carry a lot more than a few of anything.

Flavio navigated onto the 10 and lumbered along in the right lane.

"So how was Santa Barbara?" Truman said.

He laughed. "You heard about that, huh."

"Celeste and I are pretty close."

"It's important to have good friends. She's a special one. I actually like her a lot."

"I thought you were with someone else."

Flavio eyed him. "Did Celeste tell you that?"

Truman looked out the window. "It's hard to keep something like that a secret. My mentor says with matters of the heart, all bets are off." What Biff had actually written was, *Don't go soft for a dame when she gives you the big eye; it clouds your judgment and makes you a stumblebum,* but Truman's version was a reasonable synopsis of the idea.

"What's that supposed to mean?"

"Just that it's impossible to predict what people will do when they're acting on their emotions. Romantic relationships and crushes and all that."

"I might have a crush on your friend. I just find her so intriguing. What's she really like?"

Truman took a breath. "I think you've got most of the details already. She works in the art world, and grew up in East LA."

"But she doesn't speak Spanish."

"My sense is that she understands a lot more than she thinks she does."

"She's an intellectual, wouldn't you say? I find that so mysterious."

"How do you measure something like that?" Truman said. "I know she's smart, and she has a degree, if that means anything."

Flavio merged onto the 5, headed south.

"So what kind of stuff are we moving?" Truman said.

"Fabric and some finished garments. You'll see soon enough."

Exiting the freeway in the sprawling warehouse district of Commerce, Flavio maneuvered the oversize vehicle on the wide streets, plied mostly by even larger semitrucks with trailers. Eventually he slowed and turned into a gated yard.

Shipping containers were stacked all around, in some places several layers high. He backed the truck toward one that sat on its own at the side of the yard, then set the parking brake. Reaching under the seat, he produced a pair of grubby work gloves, and handed them to Truman, then climbed out.

Truman walked toward the end of the truck, tucking the gloves in the back of his belt. He'd parked it just a few feet from one end of the container, painted dull blue and stenciled with serial numbers. Flavio pressed a switch mounted on the end of the truck's box, and with an electric whine the lift gate folded open until it was flat and then slowly descended to the ground. A big metal square studded with serrations to make it less slippery, it was designed to act as an elevator platform. At least they wouldn't have to heave the stuff up to the level of the truck bed.

Stepping over to the container, Flavio glanced at his phone, then dialed a number into the combination lock. It popped open, and he pulled it off, then folded open the container doors. It was tightly packed with bolts of fabric, standing on end and shrink-wrapped in plastic.

Flavio waved at the contents. "We just have to get all this on the truck."

"That's a lot of stuff." Moving closer, Truman peered into the dim interior. "There's a weird smell. Like chemicals."

"That's probably the pesticide. They spray it inside before it leaves China."

"And we're just going to breathe it in?" he demanded.

"It'll dissipate in a minute. Come on."

He hefted up a bolt of fabric and carried it to the lift gate, setting it at the back. Truman pulled on the gloves and held his breath as he grabbed a bolt, and carried it over, and set it on the gate. Before long they had a pile of them, and Flavio waved for him to join him on the platform. When he toggled the switch, the gate slowly rose upward, and stopped when it was level with the bed of the truck. They shifted all the bolts into the box, then lowered the gate again and started to move another load from the container.

Flavio hadn't said anything about paying him for this, Truman realized. He'd framed it as a favor, but this was straight-up unskilled manual labor.

Once they'd moved all the bolts, he could see what was behind them, deeper in the container:

vacuum-packed plastic bales with colorful compressed fabric visible inside.

"Is this finished clothing?" Truman said.

"Exactly. Let's get going."

Flavio heaved up a bale and carried it out to the pile on the lift gate. Copying his actions, Truman lifted one of the bundles. In its airless state it felt solid, not like fabric, more like wood or paper, and it was a lot heavier than it looked.

"This stuff is obviously not high-end if it's packed like this," he said, squatting to drop the bale on the lift gate.

"Don't worry about that. Let's just get it on the truck."

Mercifully the container was the short version, maybe half the size of the large ones, and eventually they got to the back wall. Once they'd loaded the last of the clothes, Flavio closed up the container, and rolled down the truck's back door, then folded up the lift gate.

"Are you going to unload all this at your workshop?" Truman said, climbing up into the cab.

"I have a warehouse space. It's not far."

Grateful to be sitting down, Truman let his body relax. His arms ached. He could use a beer right now.

Flavio drove west, under all the electrical lines and over the river, then turned into a retail self-storage place with squat sheet-metal units in long rows. He parked in the middle of an aisle and popped his door handle.

"This is your warehouse space?" Truman said.

"Do you have a problem with that?"

"I wouldn't have called it a warehouse."

Flavio scoffed and climbed out. "Come on."

When he unlocked the storage unit and rolled up the door, it was mostly empty, except for a few bolts of shrink-wrapped fabric propped in a corner. Truman pulled his gloves on again, and they started to unload the truck. It felt like it was going slower, that the bolts and the bales were heavier now, probably because he was getting worn out. Eventually the truck was empty, and Flavio folded up the lift gate, and snapped the padlock on the storage unit.

"Excellent work," he said, and clapped Truman on the back.

They climbed into the cab, and Truman dropped the sweaty work gloves on the floor, then sank back into the seat, letting his muscles relax. Flavio headed back onto the 5. As they rolled, Truman gazed out the window at the gritty concrete of the industrial neighborhood. Was this another audition, he wondered, with Flavio assessing his work ethic, his pliability? Maybe it was just free labor. He could demand to get paid, of course, but he wouldn't. Technically he was hanging around these people for a case, and there was more to glean from them.

Flavio interrupted his thoughts. "Listen, Truman—I wanted to tell you about Huck. He has to focus right now."

"What do you mean?"

"He needs to work on building our business." He glanced at Truman and waved a hand. "He doesn't need to be messing around with guys who'll just dump him when the fun is over."

Truman frowned. "You're not his father, are you? It seems to me what Huck and I get up to falls into the category of not your business."

Flavio chuckled. "It is my business. I need him at the top of his game. He's like family to me, and I have every right to protect him."

"Why does he need protecting?" Truman threw up his hands. "It's not like he's nine years old. He manages to navigate the world pretty well on his own."

"All I'm saying is, there's plenty of guys in this town. You don't need to mess with Huck."

"What about Celeste? How would you feel if I told you to stay away from her?"

He laughed. "She's not a simple person. She's a highly skilled diplomat."

And you're a patriarchal buffoon, Truman thought, but he didn't say that. "I assume you're talking about Celeste dealing with Alicia's anger. Rightfully that should have been directed at you."

"Oh, Truman—you don't sleep with them. You have no idea what women are like. I need to stay out of that part of it."

Truman huffed and looked out the window, and they rode in silence for a while.

"I need to return this truck on Alameda,"

Flavio said. "Can you get home from there? It's not far from downtown."

Truman looked over at him. "You can drop me at my place. Right where you picked me up."

"All right. I guess it's not that far out of my way." When Flavio pulled up in front of his building, he beamed at him and said, "Thanks for your help today."

"OK," Truman said evenly, briefly holding his gaze.

"Get some rest," he called after him as he stepped out.

Ignoring that, Truman slammed the door and went upstairs.

SIXTEEN

EDITING THE PATTERN IMAGES to remove the branding was tedious, but not difficult, Celeste found. It was mostly about cropping off the sides where the printing was or deleting the layers with the other companies' logos. Even the images with watermarks weren't locked, so it was easy to just delete the overlay.

Alicia took a couple of phone calls but mostly stared at her screen. Huck came into the back room for a while and worked on the computer at the third desk, and then left again.

Once she was certain no one was going to come and look over her shoulder, Celeste clicked around in the cloud drive to see what else she could find. Even though she had access to the drive, all the other folders in it were locked, demanding a password. It wasn't easy to set up that kind of fragmented security, she thought, staring at the password pop-up. Eurorapt definitely had things to hide.

———·———

ONCE TRUMAN HAD A shower, he felt too hot to get dressed, so he pulled on a clean pair of underpants, and made an espresso, and ate some fruit. The more he thought it through, the angrier he got.

Flavio had taken advantage of him. It was the same way he treated Huck. Flavio knew that Truman didn't have any income right now, since he'd quit the fabric store, so he'd marked him for labor rather than exploiting him for cash, like the gallery owner he went after in Santa Barbara, pressing him to buy into his crypto scheme. Flavio was a damn chiseler.

At his desk, Truman pulled open his laptop and looked up Neil Nephard's business. It was repped by showrooms in New York and LA, but the office was in the Fashion District, and it wasn't far away—he could walk there.

He pulled on a clean shirt, and his green jeans, and a light nylon jacket, then went down the stairs and set off.

From the street Neil's office looked a little like the Eurorapt office, an aging ground-level commercial building, but it was bigger. He tried the door, and found it unlocked, and stepped inside.

Buyers for retailers usually saw clothing

collections at the showrooms in the Mart on Main Street, Truman knew, but Neil also had some samples on display here. A pair of big-breasted headless gray mannequins were clad in colorful minimalist bikinis, flanked by a couple of the male version, with massive pecs, in high-cut swimsuits that were just as revealing. Clearly Neil was an equal-opportunity exposer of flesh.

At the desk farther inside was a woman with dark hair piled up in a messy bundle. She looked at him over her thick glasses.

"Can I help you?"

"I wanted to talk to Neil."

"Do you have an appointment?"

"I don't," Truman said, "but you could tell him I'm researching an intellectual property case."

She frowned. "If it involves a legal matter, you should contact the company's lawyers."

"It's not about anything legal. It concerns Neil's design process."

"Do you have a business card?"

He dug one out of his hip pocket and stepped over to her desk to hand it to her. She read it, then eyed him, her brow furrowing. It bore only his contact details and his name, with the word INVESTIGATIONS printed below it, providing no association with any recognizable organization, or even a profession, so it was no surprise that she looked dubious.

"It might be better for you to talk to the business manager," she said. "Her office is at the factory on Eleventh."

"Is Neil here today? I only need a few minutes of his time."

She pursed her lips, but then rose from her chair and stepped toward the chic frosted-glass door in the back wall. "Give me a minute."

As she stepped out, pulling the door closed behind her, Truman ogled the mannequins. They were extremely buff, with six-pack muscles, the tight little swimsuits stacked way beyond any semblance of reality. That had to be a lot of the power the fashion business had to get people to spend, he realized—the aspiration to this kind of impossible ideal.

The woman returned a minute later and called to him, "He'll be with you in a moment."

As she sat at her desk, Truman saw that she didn't have his card in hand any longer.

The door into the back swung open, and Neil strode out. Truman recognized him from his portrait. He was older now, dressed in a black turtleneck and loose jeans, and wore thick-rimmed glasses. That was a familiar tactic among performers and fashion types: when you hit a certain age, glasses made you look younger.

He'd lost the frosted look, and his hair was totally blond now. He could almost pull it off, Truman saw, as his dark roots were partly gray.

Neil smiled at him as he approached. "You're lucky to find me here. I was in New York last week. I might have to go again soon."

"I'm glad I caught you," Truman said, and gestured to the mannequins. "I've been admiring your work. It's so beautiful."

Neil made a little bow from the neck, acknowledging the compliment, but in a routine way, like he heard that a lot.

"So what can I do for you today?"

Truman eyed the clerk at the desk. Even though she was ignoring them, he said, "It's somewhat confidential. Can I buy you a coffee?"

Neil pointedly looked him up and down. "A strapping young man like you could buy me anything you wanted."

Truman laughed. "You might need to get your glasses checked."

"Come along, then. We'll go to the French place on the corner."

He led the way out the front door, and they walked up the block, Truman matching his confident pace.

"Your card said your name is Boudreaux," Neil said. "I knew a Cajun fellow from Lafayette, Louisiana, with that name."

"No relation. My people are from Massachusetts."

"It also said 'investigations,'" he said, eyeing him sidelong. "You don't look like a PI. Do you have a gun under that TPU-laminated nylon?"

"I'm not licensed, and I'm not packing a heater." Truman pulled open the tails of his jacket. "I'm more like a researcher."

"You're definitely bringing the heat, son," he said, as they stepped into the restaurant's courtyard. Truman had to grin. He knew it wasn't personal. With some people the innuendo and the flirting were automatic.

Neil caught the server's eye, and she smiled in recognition and gestured to a table.

"You must come here a lot," Truman said as they sat down.

"I don't, but I tip well."

The woman stepped over, and Neil greeted her like an old friend.

"Can you make me a skinny latte?" he said.

"Of course." She looked to Truman, and he ordered an espresso, and she stepped away.

"So you know what I do," Neil said, folding his hands on the tabletop. "What do my colorful little *shmatte* have to do with intellectual property disputes?"

"It's not so much a dispute," Truman said. "It's more about how the industry works. I wanted to ask about how you deal with people copying your work."

"Patterns can't be copyrighted," he said, raising his eyebrows, "but prints can. Of course people make close copies of my pieces. It's how the business works."

"But a knock-off takes months to produce, doesn't it?"

"Exactly." Neil waved a hand. "By then I'm already on to the next thing."

Truman waited for the server to set down their cups.

"So there's a clear difference between your current work and the older stuff."

"The current collection is where all the energy goes, and it's where most of the sales are." Neil sipped at his latte. "We used to do it by season, but that system is changing as fashion speeds up. These days we just call them collections."

"What if someone could copy your work quickly—almost simultaneously?"

"I'd be in big trouble. It would destroy my advantage, and cheapen my product."

"Have you ever had any problem with that? People copying you in a rapid time frame?"

"Not yet." He frowned. "What exactly are you researching?"

"I'm afraid that's confidential."

Neil cracked a smile. "So mysterious."

They chatted a little more about the industry, and Neil finished his coffee and sat up.

"Thanks for talking with me," Truman said, and dug in his pants for his cash.

"I'll take care of this," Neil said, and produced a neat wad of bills held together by a gold clip.

"I said I'd buy. It's a small compensation for your time."

He waved dismissively. "This is one of the privileges of age, my boy." Peeling off two twenties, he set them on the table and put his cup on top, then rose. This place wasn't cheap, Truman knew, but that was still a very good tip.

"Come back to my office with me," Neil said. "I have something for you."

They walked the short distance back to his storefront and stepped inside.

"Give me one second," Neil said, and stepped into the back.

When he reemerged a moment later, he had a swatch of royal-blue fabric in one hand. As he approached, he tossed it underhand to Truman, who snagged it out of the air. It was a pair of underpants, he saw, folding them open. The fabric was soft, and luxy, and the size looked right.

"Would you wear them?" Neil said.

"I like the high cut because I walk a lot. I'll enjoy these."

"Good," he said, and beamed. "They're from my new collection."

"Thanks again," Truman said, and tucked the shorts into his jacket pocket as he turned to leave.

"Truman," Neil said, and waited for him to turn back. "What are you doing later?"

"Are you asking me out?"

He flashed his palms. "Just for dinner."

"You're not headed to New York?"

"Not today."

"Sure, I'll eat with you," Truman said. "My number is on my card."

Walking out to the street, he had to smile.

———·———

CELESTE SPENT MOST OF the day at Eurorapt, editing the graphics files, even though she knew it made her just as much a pirate as these grifters. Later in the afternoon she went to the gallery for a couple of hours, and returned some calls, and caught up on email. Near closing time she texted Truman:

Are you around?

His reply came soon after:

Home. Drop by.

Saffron wasn't here today, so Celeste locked up the gallery and set the alarm, then went out to the alley and climbed in her car. When she got to Truman's place, he buzzed her upstairs.

"Coffee?" Truman said.

"It's too late in the day. I'll take a soda."

She helped herself to a bottle in the fridge and twisted off the cap. Truman grabbed one too, and they went to sit on the sofas.

"You look tired," he said, and crossed his legs. "Are you OK?"

Celeste scowled at him. "You don't get to judge me. I'm totally clean."

"What did I say?"

"'Tired' is a euphemism for 'smacked out on opiates.'"

"All I meant was that you looked tired. I'm freaking tired right now. Don't bite my head off."

She waved a hand. "OK."

"Since you brought it up, how is your sobriety going?"

"Tru, I'm not a wastoid," she snapped. And louder, "I'm fine."

He jabbed his index finger in the air. "Reset. Where's the reset button? Christ. So what did they have you doing at Eurorapt?"

Celeste took a deep breath, mentally shifting gears, and told him about working on the pattern images.

"The files were from four different companies," she said. "They wanted me to trim off the logos and remove the watermarks. The reason you watermark something in the first place is to say, 'Don't copy this.'"

"So you think they're stolen."

"What other reason could there be?"

"It fits with them ripping off Yaz's fabric," Truman said. "But how are they doing it?"

"I need to get access to the rest of the cloud drive. It creeps me out to be doing this," Celeste said, gesturing with her bottle. "Helping them rip people off. But I can slow-walk it while I dig."

"It's interesting that they didn't frame it as something illicit."

"I'm sure they expected me to ask why they needed to remove someone else's logos, but I didn't."

"Flavio said you're a skilled diplomat."

She scoffed. "Him and that big buoyant ego. He let Alicia come after me, so then she and I had to figure it out. He didn't have to do any-thing—no consequences."

"Straight guys," Truman said flatly.

"They're not all like that. But yeah—straight guys. When did you talk to him?"

"Flavio put me to work today," he said, and described loading the truck and transferring the cargo.

"That's what you hire day laborers for. He didn't even offer to pay you?"

"I wasn't really upset about it until after. When I had time to think about it. I kind of just let it happen."

"What a dick." Celeste sighed. "I guess he is your target, and we know he's up to something. You can write it off as part of your research."

"I went to see Neil Nephard today. The guy who owns the house Huck broke into."

"I know who Neil Nephard is. That was his place? They call him the bard of bikinis, and the sheik of shorts."

Truman chuckled. "He does make great stuff."

"Do we think Huck was looking for patterns to steal?"

"What else? Patterns or prints. The same as how they ripped off Yaz."

"I wonder if someone broke into her com-puter too?" Celeste said.

"It might be useful to interview her again, but I kind of want to follow this through first."

"Did you tell Neil he was being jacked?"

"Not yet. I don't want it to get back to Euro-rapt. I'm actually seeing him tonight."

Her eyebrows shot up. "You asked him out? He's an important man."

"He asked me. I'm not that attracted to him. But he did give me a sweet pair of underpants from his latest collection."

"Free clothes." Celeste nodded. "That means you're obligated to sleep with him. I completely understand."

Truman laughed. "It might not get to that point. But he is kind of charming."

SEVENTEEN

A WHILE AFTER CELESTE HAD gone, as the light was fading in the sky outside his big tattersall windows, Truman's phone rang—Neil Nephard.

"There's a steakhouse on Fig," Neil said when he picked up. "I thought we could try that."

"I can't eat that kind of food," Truman said. "Do you know that brewpub on Eighth?"

"What's the name of this establishment?"

"Why don't you pick me up? I'll show you." Truman rattled off his address. "Text me when you get here and I'll come down."

He changed into the new underpants, and a pair of chinos that flattered his butt, and a clubbing shirt. His phone rang, and he pulled it out to see that it was Neil.

"I'm not sure I'm in the right place," he said.

"There are little shops on one side, and a warehouse and a homeless encampment on the other."

"That's me," Truman said. "I'll be right down."

At the curb was a rag-top black Bimmer, with the top up and the parking lights on. With the tinted windows he couldn't see inside, but the engine was running—this had to be Neil.

Pulling open the passenger door, he climbed in. Neil was wearing a tan-colored coat and a bright red-and-orange scarf. It was a cool evening, but that seemed like a lot more clothes than the temperature required.

"Please tell me you don't live in a tent in that alley," Neil said, his eyes wide.

Truman chuckled. "I live in the warehouse. Although it's not a warehouse anymore."

"I can't believe people actually live around here."

"I can't imagine living anywhere else."

"I guess you're in the thick of it, if you work for fashion people. So where are we going?"

"Up the block, and make a left on Eighth," Truman said.

He flicked on the headlights and pulled away from the curb.

"I was surprised you accepted my invitation," Neil said. "Is it because you're a little starstruck?"

"I wasn't yanking your chain when I said your work is beautiful," Truman said. "But I'm not actually all that excited about fashion. I buy most of my clothes at thrift stores."

"So why did you say yes?"

"You asked. I respect the direct approach."

"It's not because I'm rich?"

"I'm not all that excited about flash and conspicuous consumption either," Truman said.

"I guess that's why we're going to a pub and not a steakhouse," Neil said, and braked for a red light.

Truman watched him for a moment. "Why are you digging for a motive? It sounds so insecure. You're hotter than you think you are."

He reached over to slap Truman's knee. "Stop it. I'm a faded bloom. Ready to be chucked out the day after the party."

"There's other things that are just as important as how your pants fit. Manners, and charm. Confidence is a big one too. You had that going on when we went for coffee."

"Oh, Truman—you are a honey dripper."

"Park along here if you see a space. The pub is up there on the left."

When they walked into the brewpub, the screens behind the long bar were playing a football game. The host pointed them to a booth. Neil pulled off his long coat, and hung it on a hook, but left his scarf on. He was wearing a stretchy black shirt underneath.

They slid into the booth across from each other, and Neil looked around. "All these straight men. I'm getting the shivers."

"It's not like it's a small town in the South.

These are Angelenos."

He raised his eyebrows. "The type who play team sports."

"Or watch them, at least." He grinned. "It's good to step outside your comfort zone sometimes, don't you think?"

The server stepped up. "What'll it be, boys?"

Neil ordered a burger, and Truman asked for a flatbread pizza. While they waited Neil chatted about the shows in New York. It wasn't Truman's world, but it was interesting to listen to, in a way, filling in more of his understanding of the industry.

Once the food arrived, Neil waved a hand. "Anyway, it's inspiring to see all that creativity concentrated in one place."

"Winters are pretty harsh in the Northeast," Truman said, pulling his pizza apart. "There must be snow on the ground right now."

"Absolutely—but when it's cold, you can wear jackets and scarves and gloves."

"That makes sense. If you love clothes, there'd be way more opportunity to work a look."

"So what do you do besides investigating fashion crimes?" Neil said, gesturing with a french fry. "Or does that pay the bills?"

"So far I'm making a living. I used to be a tour guide."

"Are you at all computer savvy?"

"Not especially."

"Someone your age is trying to convince me

to move my cryptocurrency to the exchange that he works for. I'm not even sure how that's done."

Truman felt his heart start to pound. "You must be pretty tech-literate yourself if you're already invested in crypto."

"I didn't really do the technical part. My accountant thought I should get into it."

Truman held his gaze. "What's the name of the exchange?"

"I'm not exactly sure."

He nodded, and took a breath. "Based on what I know about crypto, you have to do your research."

"Meaning what?"

"Don't just move it around without being sure of what you're doing. Several of those exchanges have turned out to have such lax security that they were robbed blind, and others have been straight-up scams. The investors lost everything."

Neil frowned. "I don't even know how I'd research something like that. This one sounds like it's quite new. They're promising a high rate of return."

"The way crypto works, its value should be the same no matter where it's stored," Truman said intently. "It's not like a stock portfolio."

"I know that much," he said, his brow furrowing.

"Just be careful where you put your trust."

After they'd eaten, the server dropped the check on the table.

"I'll get it," Neil said.

Truman dug out his cash. "We'll split it," he said, and peeled off a twenty, and met his gaze. "I insist."

Neil pulled on his coat, and tied the belt, and they walked out to the street.

"It was lovely to get to know you a little better," Neil said, pausing on the sidewalk.

"Are you seriously calling it?" Truman waved an arm. "The night is young. I thought we might get to know each other even better. I have some tequila at my place."

"I have to be up so early. There's a video call with people back east."

"So you'll double down on coffee in the morning. And you'll have a smile on your face."

"I almost can't believe you want to do this. With me, I mean."

"Confidence, remember?" Truman said.

He bit his lip. "Do you want to come to my place?"

"Mine is closer." More than that, he was bone tired from loading Flavio's truck, and he didn't want to have to ride the metro back from Neil's neighborhood later.

They climbed into the Bimmer, and Truman told him the turns to make to navigate back to his place. When they pulled up out front, Neil leaned over the steering wheel, peering out at the neighborhood.

"Is my car going to be safe here?"

"I have a friend who'll keep an eye on it,"

Truman said. Climbing out, he walked toward the row of tents cluttering the alley. "Yo, Beretta," he called.

Neil was out of the car now, on the sidewalk, his brow furrowed in concern. "A homeless person?"

"He's also an entrepreneur. He's never let me down."

Beretta appeared from the alley, stepping out into the wan light of the streetlamps. He was wearing his heavy coat, hands jammed in his pockets against the cold.

"Another gentleman caller," Beretta said. "You have so many I can hardly keep track."

"You make me sound like a slut."

"Your word, Sunshine, not mine."

"Can you keep an eye on the Bimmer?" Truman said.

"That's a nice car. It'll cost you."

"It won't be here all night," Truman said, and dug in his pocket. "I'll give you a fin."

"Expensive automobiles require a higher level of service. In capitalism we call that the wisdom of the market."

"I'll gladly give you what you ask," Neil said, stepping closer.

Not missing a beat, Beretta eyed him and said, "Two hundred."

"No way," Truman said. "Give him a sawbuck."

"How about twenty?" Neil said, and dug out the bill.

"Fine," Beretta said flatly. "But you're killing me here."

Neil handed over the cash, and Truman led the way to his front door, twisting his key in the lock.

"You called him Beretta," Neil said, once they were inside, climbing the stairs.

"That's right."

"He's named after a handgun."

"It's probably a street name," Truman said, and pushed into his loft.

"Oh, I get it now," Neil said, looking around. "There's so much space."

"It's great, right? It's hard to heat it, though."

"You could do amazing work in here. I bet the light is perfect in the daytime."

"It is." Truman followed him to the middle of the room.

"In my salad days I would have thrived in a place like this." He waved his arms. "I'd put a cutting table right here, and sewing machines along the wall, under the windows."

"Neil," Truman said. "Focus."

He turned toward him, and raised his eyebrows. Truman grasped his arms through his coat, and pulled him close, and kissed him. Neil's mouth was kind of soft, and inert, like maybe he wasn't really into it.

Truman pulled back. "Are you OK?"

"My heart is aflutter," he said, and smiled. "No tequila?"

"Do you want tequila?"

"I want you."

Truman led him toward the bed and started to undress, tossing his pants on the floor. Neil pulled off his coat.

"You wore my briefs."

"They're extremely comfortable," Truman said, unbuttoning his shirt.

"They look perfect on you. Such a beautiful boy."

He had to grin. "You keep calling me a boy. I'm a grown man."

"Think of it from my perspective," Neil said. "You're a lot younger than I am."

He stepped over to the clothes rack to hang up his coat, and Truman reclined on the bed, watching as he methodically got undressed, and draped his shirt and trousers over the rack.

"Get over here, son," Truman called to him.

Neil laughed as he padded over. "No one's called me that in a long time. Especially someone half my age."

Truman pulled him down onto the bed, and met his mouth, and caressed his torso. Neil explored his body, running his hands over his chest and his thighs.

"Do you want to fuck me?" Truman said, squeezing his cock.

"I don't think I'm up to it."

"Can I fuck you?"

"I think we'll have to go with less intensive

activities," Neil said. "Let me smoke you."

Truman leaned back as Neil shifted down the bed, and closed his eyes as he went down on him. When he came, he grabbed Neil's head to get him to stop.

Neil shifted up beside him, caressing his chest. "That was quick."

"It's because you're so good at it," Truman said, and reached for his cock, stroking it. It took a while, with their mouths together, but eventually Neil climaxed.

Pulling the covers over his legs, Truman stretched out, and closed his eyes, and quickly drifted off, only vaguely aware of Neil getting up, and the sound of water running. He woke again when Neil spoke.

"*Eleven Steps to Becoming a Hard-Nosed Detective.*" He was sitting on the side of the bed with Biff's book, flipping through it under the bedside lamp.

"Biff Sturgis is my mentor," Truman said.

"This book is older than I am. And I don't buy green bananas anymore."

"Hard-nosed skills never go out of style."

Neil tapped the page. "At one point here he's talking about a hot tomato. If you called a woman that today on social media, you'd get shamed back to the stone age."

"Does it only mean women?" Truman shifted onto his side. "It could apply to men too. You're kind of a hot tomato."

Neil chuckled and closed the book, then leaned in to nuzzle his neck. "Can I see you again?"

"Why not?"

He rose, and pulled on his boxer shorts, and Truman struggled to stay lucid as he watched the laborious process of Neil getting dressed. Eventually he was ready, his long coat cinched at his waist, and Truman walked him to the door.

Neil held his gaze for a moment. "Good night, Truman."

EIGHTEEN

IN THE MORNING TRUMAN's muscles ached, like he'd run a foot race. It was his own fault, he knew, for going along with Flavio, but he still resented the guy, and felt stupid for doing all that work. He popped an ibuprofen and spent some time waking up, lounging on one of the sofas with an espresso and his laptop.

Researching more about cryptocurrency, he found there was a lot of hype about it changing the world. That was typical of the tech industry, where each new idea was treated like a precious reality-shifting innovation, with blue-sky promises of greater connectedness, and equality, and democracy. In reality that industry was having the opposite effect, amplifying antidemocratic forces and worsening inequality while the regulators tried to figure out what was actually happening and struggled to catch up. Reading about it, crypto felt like that, a weed that was growing wild, at least for now, causing impacts that were hard to assess, potentially deepening the rents in the social fabric.

The analytical journalism about crypto was more rational. One analyst at a financial news site compared it to any other high-risk investment, and pointed out that the promise of making governments obsolete was a laughable pipe dream. In reality governments were starting to regulate it like any other asset.

Eventually Truman called Celeste, glad that she picked up.

"I'll swing by," she said. "I'm not far away."

A few minutes later she rang the bell, and he buzzed her up. When she walked in, she had several bulky canvases tucked under her arm.

Truman closed the door behind her. "Are those for me?"

"No," she said flatly. "I didn't want to leave them in my car."

Celeste set them against the arm of the nearest sofa. The top one was a painting of a sad clown, Truman saw, with a downturned mouth and exaggerated teardrops outlined on his white grease-painted face.

"You went back to that gallery."

"The show just closed. These cost half what they wanted for them a week ago."

Truman stooped to flip through them. They were all similarly lurid. "If any of these cost more than ten bucks, you got ripped off."

"I'm delivering them to Mariam later."

"What's your markup with her?"

Celeste pursed her lips and thought about it. "It depends, but on this kind of stuff, double or triple. Sometimes more."

"Right on. You'll make ten or twenty dollars on each of these sad idiots."

"I'm not going to tell you what they actually cost," she said, raising her eyebrows. "You'll get upset. Hook me up with some java?"

Truman went to start the espresso machine, and Celeste sat on the purple sofa.

"How was your evening with Neil?"

"He's quite charming," Truman said, over the noise of the machine. Once he'd poured the steaming joe into two little cups, he carried them over, handing her one before he sat on the adjacent sofa.

"I can't believe you slept with that guy."

"He's hot enough, but honestly, the sex was underwhelming."

"He's a cold fish?" she said, sipping at her cup.

"It was more like, 'Don't muss my hair.'"

She laughed. "It doesn't sound very erotic if you didn't need to fix your do after."

"So I think Huck is trying to get Neil to invest in Flavio's crypto exchange."

"Is that why he broke into the guy's house?"

"That was about clothes. I saw him copying image files."

"So maybe it's both," she said. "Clothes and crypto. Eurorapt are broad-spectrum crooks."

"I spent the morning reading about crypto."

She waved a hand and sat back. "Lay it on me."

"It's not really regulated yet, so there's no deposit insurance like with savings accounts. If you give it to the wrong person, it just might be gone."

"You mean the wrong exchange?"

He nodded. "Several crypto exchanges have crashed, and they get robbed pretty routinely. The biggest one in the world might actually be a pyramid scheme. Nobody's quite sure yet. It's easy to give them your coin, but people seem to have a lot of trouble getting it back."

"Who's running it?"

"No one knows. It's based in some regulation-free Caribbean island tax shelter."

"That alone smells scammy."

"Crypto mining uses more electricity than most nations," Truman went on. "The miners have bought up so much computer hardware that it caused worldwide shortages."

"So it's contributing to climate change. Delightful."

"In a big way. There's also a misperception about it being broad-based and accessible. Most coins are owned by very few people. Usually their creators. Doesn't that reek of a grift too?"

"What about the anonymity part of it?"

"The exchanges try to hide the identity of

the crypto owners, but of course they have to keep records of who they are. There are tools that crooks can use to launder their crypto and conceal their identity, but the feds seem to be able to de-anonymize it without any trouble. I'm not sure exactly how that works. The technical part of it is above my head."

Celeste waved a hand. "So crypto is shady, and the exchanges aren't regulated."

"It's pretty much the Wild West. Whatever Flavio is doing with cryptocurrency, I'm thinking it's probably bunco. He's that guy."

"We're also pretty sure Eurorapt is stealing intellectual property from other designers."

"That's what Huck was doing."

"That's what I saw yesterday at Eurorapt too." She gestured with her cup. "Now we just need to figure out how they're doing it."

"With Neil, it's about Huck," Truman said. "Neil either entrusted him with access to his house and his computer, or Huck somehow got the information from him without his knowledge."

"The way they're doing it has to be in their files, don't you think?" Celeste said. "I'm so close. I need to get Flavio to trust me enough to let me see more."

"So you're going back to Eurorapt?"

"I'll go today," she said, and got up.

———·———

Celeste carried the sad clown paintings down to her car and drove to Eurorapt. In the alley the gate to the little yard was open but the Jag was absent. Climbing out, she left the canvases in the backseat with the windows cracked. They'd be a lot safer parked back here than they would have been in Truman's grungy neighborhood.

When she pounded on the back door, Alicia pulled it open, and flashed a smile in greeting. She seemed genuinely happy to see her, not on edge anymore. Maybe the man trouble had evaporated.

Alicia was the only one here, she saw, working at her computer. Once Celeste got settled at Flavio's desk, and fired up the design programs, she turned and spoke to Alicia.

"I need to get access to some files that are in locked folders."

"I thought you had all those images," she said, her brow furrowing.

"The software keeps saying that some linked files missing, and that I need permission to access them. Sometimes a graphic file has components that are in other files."

"I suspect Flavio is more confident about his computer abilities than he should be."

"I can get to most of it," Celeste said. "It's just a few of them that won't pull up all the elements."

"Is it asking for a login?"

"Take a look." Celeste double-clicked on one of the locked folders, and rolled her chair back.

Alicia rose and leaned on the desk, peering at

the screen. "That's the cloud drive. The dummy told me he pulled everything into a local folder."

"Not everything."

Alicia huffed and pulled the keyboard closer, and rapidly typed a string of characters into the password field. She did it with one finger, so even from a few feet away, watching closely, Celeste could follow the sequence: W-E-R-E-F-A-M-O-U-S. Alicia had said that at the fashion show: "We're famous."

As Alicia stepped back, Celeste clicked on another subfolder. It opened without further protest, revealing a list of its contents.

"It looks like that worked."

Alicia sat at her desk again, and Celeste clicked around the cloud drive. She had full access to it now, it seemed. There was a lot of stuff. At least it appeared to be organized. Taking a deep breath to steady her nerves, she dived in.

Eventually she found a set of folders that bore the names of a dozen different designers. One was Feel the Trend—that shop in Hollywood. In the folder were image files like the ones she'd been working on. It was the garment that Gavin, the manufacturer they'd met, had described, she realized—a V-neck top with long tails. Somehow Eurorapt had acquired the original pattern.

The folder for Neil Nephard contained a dozen files, and when she opened them, they were patterns for swimwear pieces along with print designs for fabrics. Like Yaz's print, this was definitely someone else's intellectual property. Finding it here meant it had been stolen.

Another folder, named "Persian Woman," caught her eye. When she clicked into it, and opened the first design file, she felt her heart start to pound. It was Yaz's paisley print. Yaz had said that the bolt of fabric at A Touch of Class was a very close copy of her work—of course it was, if Eurorapt had the original design file.

She glanced sidelong at Alicia, but she was engrossed in her own thing, ignoring her. Celeste felt the sweat beading on her brow, but she pushed her anger down, shifting focus back to the screen. She opened the next file in the folder. It was another vibrant print design, and then another. When she checked the metadata, all of them had Yaz's name in the "Creator" field.

The last file was smaller, and she clicked to open it. A scan of a receipt from a company called Park Mills, with a street address in this neighborhood. It would be easy enough to email this to herself, but that would leave traces on Flavio's computer. She pulled out her phone and did a quick search for that name. Park Mills was a fabric manufacturer. This is who'd produced Yaz's fabric.

Celeste sat back and stared at the screen. The receipt was unequivocal—Eurorapt had paid someone to turn Yaz's design into that bolt of fabric. There was also hard evidence here that they were ripping off other designers. But how were they doing it?

"How is it going?" Alicia said, looking over at her. "You look stuck."

"Just taking a mental health break," Celeste said, and sat up.

Peering at the screen again, she clicked through other folders. There was lots of accounting stuff on dozens of spreadsheets. Eventually she found one named "Logins." Opening the sheet, she found a list of people's names accompanied by login credentials—user names and PINs and passwords. One column contained notes, like "office PC," and "bank," and next to Neil Nephard's name, "home PC." The file name wasn't very subtle—it implied that Flavio wasn't hiding this from Alicia and Huck. They were all in on it.

It was too risky to take a photo of this, with Alicia sitting right there. Taking slow breaths to stay calm, she kept searching, opening more of the folders. Buried in one of them was a sub-folder called "Crypto." The file at the top of the list was a text document. A template for an email message to crypto customers, she saw when she opened it:

Please provide login details for ___. I know it might seem risky, but Eurorapt will only use your credentials once to set up your cryptocurrency tracking account. After that, we'll delete the information.

And there it was—the other end of the scam. They were targeting fashion-industry people as clients for the crypto exchange, then using access to their accounts to steal their designs.

The door to the alley swung open, and Flavio stepped in, greeting them in his loud blustery voice. "How's everyone?"

Looking up at him, Celeste made a subtle keystroke to switch to one of the image-editing programs and hide what she'd been doing in the cloud drive.

"Drudgery," she said, "but it's happening."

"There weren't all that many files."

"Some of it's more technical than just cropping the images."

"Like what?" he said, his hands on his hips, raising his eyebrows.

"Like, why would I explain it to you?" she said, holding his gaze. "That's why you brought me in, isn't it? My technical skills. Sometimes you just have to leave it to your people. Let them do the work."

He laughed. "I guess that's fair. I know you're not here to steal from me."

She scoffed and looked back to the screen. "You sound paranoid."

Flavio turned to Alicia. "We should go talk to that guy."

"Right." Alicia got up, and grabbed her bag, a faint frown on her face. The pair of them went out the back door, slamming it behind them.

If Alicia told him that she'd given Celeste the cloud drive password, Flavio would be back here in a hurry to toss her out on her ear. She needed to work fast. Pulling up the spreadsheet with the login credentials again, she took a photo of it with her phone, then opened the "Crypto" folder and photographed the note soliciting them.

There had to be more, she knew, and eyed the door to the alley. They might be gone for a while, but then again, they might not. She clicked through other folders as quickly as she could, trying to parse the contents without getting bogged down. In a subfolder called "Documentation" she found dozens of records of crypto transactions, along with receipts and bank account statements. The bank was in the Cayman Islands, she saw— the mother of all offshore tax-avoidance jurisdictions.

The meaning of some of the documents wasn't clear, as they were written in the arcane language of finance and contracts, but she spent a minute scanning through the pages of one of the files that was in plain language. It was the record of a wallet that had been set up at a Bahamas-based crypto exchange.

A wallet just meant an account, she knew, and the initial transfer into the new account was 3.4 bitcoin. On her phone she did a quick search. The value of the coin fluctuated wildly, but if that were converted into dollars today, it would be worth over two hundred grand.

Even more interesting was that the account was in Huck's name. Eurorapt wasn't mentioned anywhere, and neither was Flavio, or Alicia. Clicking back through the other documents, she saw that it was the same with the Cayman bank account statements and the more complex documents, the ones whose purpose wasn't clear—they only bore Huck's name.

Celeste sat back and rubbed her eyes. What did that mean? It seemed unusual, given that Flavio was the boss of everything and everyone. She photographed some of the pages, the wallet documentation and some of the bank account documents, and then the pilfered clothing patterns and prints, then tucked her phone away, and exited the cloud drive folders, and killed all the design software. Double-checking that she hadn't left anything open, she locked the computer with a keystroke, and stood up, and stretched.

There was no way to lock this office with Flavio and Alicia gone, she realized. Had Huck wandered through earlier? She stepped into the front room, but no one was here. No way was she going to wait around for them. Stepping out to the alley, she pushed the door closed and climbed into her car.

A few blocks away, far from the security camera over Eurorapt's back door, she pulled over at a yellow curb, in front of a shuttered warehouse, and dug out her phone to call Truman.

"We need to talk," she said when he picked up.

"I'm at the library. Do you want to meet at that coffee place on Fifth?"

NINETEEN

THIS WAS A TIGHT neighborhood to find parking during office hours, but it was almost the end of the day, and Celeste found a street space right around the corner, and fed the meter. When she walked into the coffeehouse, Truman was already here, at a table near the window, with an espresso in front of him and a cup waiting for her.

She scanned the room, making sure she didn't recognize any of the other patrons, and walked over to sit across from him.

"You look a little rattled," Truman said.

"I saw some of Eurorapt's trashy secrets today."

He grinned. "You convinced Flavio to give you access to their files?"

"Alicia did." Celeste told him what she'd

found, and her theory about how they acquired access to their victims' computers, using the crypto exchange as a ruse to get login details, and then pilfered any potentially profitable design files.

Truman laughed and held up his hand. "That's amazing. You did it."

Celeste slapped his palm. "I took lots of photos. There was a folder with Yaz's work, and Neil's, and Feel the Trend. It's all there."

"So they're just basic thieves."

"There's more to it," Celeste said, wrapping her hands around her tepid cup. "About the crypto exchange. I saw some of the paperwork. I couldn't understand it all, the documents written in legalese, but it looks to me like whatever crypto they have is in a single account at an overseas exchange."

"You mean it's just a crypto wallet?" Truman said. "Flavio's not running his own exchange?"

"Not from what I saw. The way I heard Flavio explain it to his mark, it sounded like it was more diverse—that he'd set up relationships with different banks. But I didn't see anything like that."

"I guess it's no surprise that he's lying about it."

Her brow furrowed. "The other odd thing is that the wallet and all the paperwork are in Huck's name. I didn't see Eurorapt, or Flavio, or Alicia named in any of it."

"Interesting." Truman frowned and sipped his espresso.

"The initial deposit into that wallet was a few hundred grand," Celeste said, "but that was a while ago. There's no record of what's in it now."

"One of the things I read this morning is that there's a couple of websites that keep track of what's in every crypto wallet."

"How is that possible?"

"The whole thing runs on a public ledger," he said, "so it's public information. The sites are just compiling it."

"Can you search by the owner's name?"

"Those aren't public, so no—but the wallets are numbered. Do you think the photos you took will have that detail?"

"Probably." Celeste pulled out her phone and swiped through the images. Zooming in on one, she handed it to Truman. "It's not exclusively numbers, but that looks like the wallet's ID, doesn't it?"

Truman pulled out his own phone, and found one of the websites that listed wallet holdings. Once he'd typed in the lengthy string of numbers and letters, referring to the image on Celeste's phone, he ran a search for it.

"It exists in this database," he said, peering at the screen. "That particular wallet has 98.2 bitcoins in it."

Celeste grabbed her phone and did a quick conversion. "In real money that's just over six million bucks."

"Dang." Truman clicked his tongue. "No way

is that their own dough. They're putting what they've taken from other people in that wallet."

"It's a sizeable haul," she said. "Way more than the fashion stuff is worth. It would take ages to make that much money with knock-off sportswear."

"That means crypto has to be their primary game."

"I wonder if the fashion work is just to obscure the main grift?"

"Or maybe one led to the other." Truman sat up. "It's time to call Neil and tell him not to invest with these crooks. The way he talked about it last night, he was still trying to make up his mind."

"Tell him to change his passwords too. All his details were in that spreadsheet. And don't let him talk to Flavio—he'll figure out what I was up to."

"Good idea." Truman drained his little cup. "Do you want to come with?"

"Do I?" Celeste sat back and took a breath, considering that. Now that she'd shared her discoveries, she was finally starting to relax, and felt calmer. "I actually can't. I'm seeing Mariam tonight. I need a break anyway—this detective work is intense."

"You're delivering the clown paintings."

"And she's taking me to a soroptimist event."

He stood up. "Come on—I'll walk you to your car."

When they got out to the sidewalk, Truman

said, "What's a soroptimist?"

"I think it's a volunteer nonprofit kind of thing. Mariam compared it to the Rotary or the Shriners, but it's just for women." She pointed the way to the side street where she'd parked.

"Is it like Freemasonry," Truman said, walking abreast, "where there's a bunch of secret rituals?"

"I guess I'll find out."

"If it's all secret, you might not even be able to tell me."

"So I guess you'll never know for sure." As they approached her car, Celeste leaned in for an air kiss.

"Amazing work," Truman said. "You totally cracked it."

She grinned and stepped around to the driver's door. "At least we got something for Yaz."

Truman pulled out his phone, walking toward the metro station, and called Neil, glad that he picked up.

"I need a few minutes of your time," Truman said. "Can I drop by your house?"

"I'd planned on an early evening. We're talking now—what's up?"

"I wanted to talk in person."

"You kept me up so late last night."

"You poor thing," Truman said. "Hot sex is such a chore."

Neil laughed. "Can you tell me what's so important, at least?"

"Not on the phone. It won't take long."

"The hard-nosed detective is so mysterious. You're not going to try to borrow money from me, are you?"

"I don't need your damn money, man," he said, raising his voice.

"Don't get steamed. Sure—come over, if you must."

"I'll be there in half an hour."

"You don't know where I live."

"You told me you lived in Hancock Park," Truman said quickly. "What's the street address?"

That was a ham-handed slip, he thought, as he trotted down the stairs into the metro. No wonder the guy was suspicious of him.

He rode the train west and walked to Neil's neighborhood from Wilshire. It was farther than he'd thought, and even though it was already dark out, and getting colder, by the time he turned onto Neil's street he'd worked up a sweat.

Truman went to the front entrance, rather than the side door that Huck had gone in, and rang the bell. When Neil opened it, he was wearing a wildly colorful kimono with a bird-of-paradise print.

"That was a very long half hour."

"I love that print," Truman said.

Neil stepped back and held up his arm, revealing more of the green-and-orange fabric on the voluminous sleeve. "Come in." As he led the way through to the kitchen, he said, "I made a pitcher of caipirinhas. Can I pour your one?"

"Those are sweet, right?" Truman ran a hand through his hair to disperse the sweat. "What the hell. Set me up."

Neil waved him to a barstool, and Truman sat and watched as he put ice cubes in a tumbler, then poured the cocktail from a pitcher.

"This is mint. It's edible." He stuck a little green leaf in the glass and slid it across to him. "So what was so urgent that you needed to see me tonight?"

"Cheers," Truman said, and clinked his glass against Neil's, then took a sip. It was tart and sweet and tasty. "You need to change your computer password."

Neil frowned. "Why?"

"You're being hacked. That crypto opportunity you talked about is bogus."

"And how would you know that?"

"The guy who pitched it to you is named Huck."

His eyebrows shot up. "Do you know him?"

"Huck is part of the con operation I'm investigating. They're targeting fashion industry players."

"Huck introduced me to the CEO of the exchange."

"Flavio?" Truman waved an arm. "He's not the CEO of anything, except maybe his own ego."

"You said 'con.' What kind of con?"

"They have your login details, don't they?"

"I haven't given them anything yet," Neil said.

"Although Flavio said he'd need some information to move my crypto into his exchange."

"Well, somehow Huck already knows how to get into your computer. Ergo, you need to change your password."

"How do you know this?"

"We can get into that later. Right now, why not just change the password? Whether I'm right or I'm way off base, you have nothing to lose."

Neil stared at him for a moment. "Can they get into it remotely?"

"I'm not sure."

"I'll do it now." He scooped up his tumbler and strode toward the office at the back of the house. "I have so many questions, Truman," he called back.

Following him, Truman stood in front of the desk and watched as Neil sat down, and took a slurp of his cocktail, then pulled on a pair of reading glasses and peered at the computer screen.

"Thank you for believing me," Truman said.

He briefly glanced up at him over his glasses. "I don't know Huck very well."

"Don't talk to him again, and don't deal with Flavio either."

Neil was typing now, focused on the screen. Finally he sat back. "I think that's done it."

"Do you know how to change the code for your burglar alarm? The one for this house."

His eyes grew wide. "They know that too?"

"Think about it—did you give it to Huck, or

did he have an opportunity to see you use it?"

Neil's brow furrowed, and he looked away, considering that. "I'll call the alarm company," he said finally. "So how exactly are they scamming people?"

"I can't explain that now. There are still some moving parts. I know I'm repeating myself, but don't talk to them again, and don't give them any-thing—passwords or bitcoins or money."

"I know how to be discreet, my boy. I was gay during the darkest depths of the 1970s." He waved dismissively. "If any of this is true, how long until you wrap it up and call in the authorities?"

"It is true," Truman said intently. "Has Flavio moved any of your crypto to his exchange?"

"I didn't initiate that yet." He met Truman's eye. "He didn't seem like a crook to me. And Huck was so earnest."

"Of course he was. That's how cons work." Truman frowned. "If you don't believe me, why did you just change your password?"

"Like you said, there was nothing to lose in doing that. But if you're right, I have a lot to lose." He held Truman's gaze. "I wish you'd explain yourself. If they know how to get into my com-puter, and they know my alarm code, I want to know exactly what other information they've taken from me."

"I can't discuss the details yet," Truman said. "I wanted to give you a heads up so they couldn't get anything else."

"But that'll happen at some point? The revelation of actual evidence?"

"It will, Neil." He sighed. "Sometimes you just have to trust the process."

"I run a business. I'm not used to not being in control."

"Let me get my drink," Truman said, and walked back to the kitchen.

Neil followed him, and refilled his own tumbler from the pitcher.

"This is all quite intriguing," Neil said, swirling the contents of his glass. "I'm struggling not to be suspicious of you."

"I guess I can understand that." Truman perched on a barstool. "You don't really know me. But I'm doing you a favor here, at the risk of blowing up my own investigation."

"You also didn't ask to see my passwords or access my computer yourself. That's somewhat reassuring." He sipped his cocktail and set the glass on the counter. "I was supposed to talk to Flavio this week."

"Just stall him," Truman said intently. "No matter what he says."

Neil dropped his chin and held his gaze. "Can you stay?"

"I thought you had to be up early again."

"It might be worth it."

Truman shook his head. "I should go."

"Because I'm too swishy?" Neil scowled and waved his arms, the long kimono sleeves billowing. "The boy in a dress?"

The guy was more inebriated than he'd thought, Truman realized. He was either a lightweight or he'd been drinking before he got here.

"You're no boy, toots, and a kimono isn't a dress." Truman threw up his hands. "You're also making assumptions about me. I actually like swishy guys."

Neil frowned. "Why?"

"They usually have fewer hang-ups."

He cracked a smile. "So stay."

Truman thought about it for a moment. "No more booze for me, then, if we're going to get busy."

Neil clapped his hands, then led him upstairs, into a bedroom with a big canopy bed. The thick burgundy drapes on the windows matched the fabric hanging at the corners of the bed. Neil spent a lot of time running his hands over Truman's body, and Truman went with it. Even with lowered expectations, this was hot, and it took some time, but they built up to a climax.

Later, Truman woke from dozing. Neil was snoring, he realized, and the sound had pulled him into consciousness. It was subtle, maybe just booze-induced apnea from the caipirinhas, but he couldn't sleep with that going on. Quietly getting dressed, he went downstairs and let himself out.

TWENTY

T HE BUZZ OF THE doorbell woke Truman in the morning. He was in his own bed, he realized, and the memory of coming home last night flooded into his mind. The buzzer sounded again, and he jumped up and went over to answer.

It was Celeste, and he buzzed her up, and flipped open the deadbolt, then hustled over to his clothes rack to pull on a pair of sweatpants and a T-shirt.

"I woke you," Celeste said, stepping in and closing the door.

"I should have been up. Do you want some coffee?" He went to the counter and fumbled with the espresso machine.

"How was Neil?" Celeste said. "Did he flip out about being hacked?"

"He took it in stride. At least he took it seriously enough to change his passwords."

"Did you sleep with him again?"

"No comment," Truman said. "How were the soroptimists?"

"I can't say, except that they definitely know how to party."

"I knew it." He handed her a little steaming cup of espresso. "You can't say because it's a secret society."

"I could tell you that," she said, once she'd taken a sip, "but only if you took that drug that wipes out your short-term memory first."

"It's called Versed," Truman said. "But I'm not sure I want to know badly enough."

"I think we need to go talk to the manufacturer who jacked Yaz's fabric. Park Mills. It's right near here."

"Let's do it," he said. "I also want to warn the woman at the store in Hollywood, like I warned Neil. That might be more time-sensitive."

"You want to go up there first?" Celeste said. "You'll love the clothes."

"Not if everything is a size 2 and smaller."

"I didn't notice that. The owner isn't a size 2 and she wears her own stuff. It's eclectic and earthy."

He slurped at the steaming java, then set the cup down, and went over to his clothes rack to get dressed.

A minute later they headed down to the

street, and climbed into Celeste's car, and got on the freeway. Once she'd exited in Hollywood, Truman pointed out the storefront of Feel the Trend, and she nosed into a metered street space.

When they walked into the shop, Celeste immediately got distracted by the clothes, and stopped to look through a rack of blouses. Truman walked toward the back, and soon found Rocky, again dressed in an earthy brown top from the store's merchandise.

Rocky smiled in recognition. "It's my landlord-meeting wing man."

"Have you invested with Flavio yet?" he said.

Her brow furrowed. "I just talked to him yesterday. He says he needs a commitment from me soon."

"Don't give him anything. Dollars or crypto. And change your computer password."

"I already gave him access to my cloud drive."

"You need to undo that," Truman said intently. "Like, now."

"What's going on?"

"I don't know all the details yet, but I know he's running a scam."

"Like a pyramid scheme?"

"I'm not sure how it works. They're thieves, Rocky."

"Flavio said getting in at this point will be hugely profitable for me. If I wait, I'll lose out."

"What con job doesn't start out with a pitch like that?" Truman demanded. "Think about it."

"What evidence do you have?"

"There's nothing tangible that I can show you right now, but there will be."

"So I just have to take your word?"

Truman ran a hand through his hair and took a breath. "Rocky, I'm trying to help you."

"What's your connection to Flavio?"

"Someone else that he conned hired me to look into it."

"All right." She nodded. "I'll take your warning under advisement."

He threw up his hands. "Do what you want. But whatever you do, please don't tell him you talked to me."

"Why not?"

"Because it'll blow up my investigation. Can you at least do that for me?"

"Fine. I won't mention the mysterious Truman Boudreaux."

It was impressive that she'd remembered his surname, he thought, as he walked back toward the front of the store. He found Celeste flicking through garments hanging on a rack.

"There's some nice pieces here," she said.

"Are you going to buy anything?"

"Not today."

"Can we go?"

She followed him out to the street.

"This was a mistake," Truman said. "She doesn't believe me."

"Why not?"

"She bought into Flavio's sales pitch."

Celeste stepped around to the driver's door. "When people believe something, it's hard to change their minds. Especially if there's a personal relationship. It's like trying to turn a freight train around."

"Flavio is going to rob her blind." Truman climbed in and took a breath.

"At least you tried. Is she going to rat you out to Flavio?"

"I asked her not to. I guess we'll see."

Celeste pulled into the street and headed back to the freeway. On the way to the Fashion District they talked about how they were going to approach the manufacturer.

Navigating with his phone, Truman pointed out the address for Park Mills. It was on the edge of the neighborhood, where it got more industrial, and the building looked gritty, a windowless whitewashed brick wall flush to the sidewalk. The business was identified by a small sign on a pedestrian door, next to a wider steel shutter that was rolled down and padlocked. When Truman twisted the door handle, it was unlocked.

They stepped into a small office with worn blue carpet and a desk with nobody sitting at it. Their arrival must have been noticed, however, or triggered a sensor, as a moment later they heard a door close somewhere deeper inside, and a man stepped out of the hallway.

He had thick black hair, cut a little long for his

age, and wore a navy-blue suit without a necktie.

"What can I do for you?" he said, and smiled.

"I have a clothing line," Celeste said, "and I wanted to talk about getting my print milled."

"Then I'm your guy. The name is Park."

"I'm Penelope," she said, "and this is Truman."

"Come into my office."

He led them into the hallway and an even smaller office, where they sat across the desk from him, close together on armless chairs.

"What kind of material do you need to produce?" Park said, leaning back.

"I've already designed the print," Celeste said. "What kind of fabric can you work with?"

"Cotton, and lots of the synthetics, and the blends." He made a wide gesture. "Whatever you need."

"What's your production time frame?"

"I have the milling and dyeing done in Korea and then shipped back. If it's a big order it'll come by sea, but if it's just a few bolts I can fly them back. Maybe six weeks."

Celeste eyed Truman, and he sat up.

"You manufactured a bolt of fabric for a company named Eurorapt," he said.

"Sure—I work with Flavio sometimes."

"It's this one." Truman pulled up an image of Yaz's paisley and held it out toward Park.

"I remember it. We made a bolt of cotton-poly blend in that print."

"Eurorapt doesn't own the copyright to this.

Does that matter to you?"

Park's eyebrows shot up. "Who are you, exactly?"

"I'm investigating the copyright issue," Truman said, and stood up briefly to hand his business card across the desk.

Park glanced at it, then set it down. "I wouldn't knowingly violate someone's copyright."

"Well, you did."

"If what you say is true, actually Eurorapt did. I'm just a subcontractor." He shrugged. "All I have is your word. From my perspective, Eurorapt seems legit."

"What if I brought you evidence that they don't have the rights to the design?"

"That's what the court system is for. Let the lawyers dig through it."

"You're right," Celeste said. "That's the mechanism for resolving this kind of dispute. But we'll do you a favor if you do us a favor."

Park chuckled and waved for her to continue. He wasn't at all intimidated, Truman saw, just amused at their attempt to sway him.

"You don't tell Flavio we're investigating him, and we'll keep your company out of any legal tangle."

He nodded. "Lawyers are expensive, and I haven't heard from Flavio in months, so that's easy. It's a deal." He watched her for a moment. "Are you the copyright owner?"

"My client is," Truman said. "Penelope is

assisting me in my inquiries."

Park eyed her. "Do you even have a clothing line?"

"I don't," she said, feeling her face heating up. "That was just a way to get in the door. I didn't want to lead with accusing you of something."

"Fraud," he said, raising his eyebrows. "You're accusing me of fraud."

Truman waved a hand. "Like you said, my sense is that Flavio is the fraudster."

"Can you tell me about that screen?" Celeste said, gesturing to it. Filling the wall behind his desk were three hinged panels, painted gold and framed in black, depicting a medieval Asian scene with mountains and pine trees and a human figure next to an oxcart.

"It's a reproduction of a historical piece," Park said, not looking at it. "The original is invaluable. You can get these in Seoul for a few hundred dollars."

"Would you be willing to hook me up with a supplier?"

"I don't know any, but I bought that at a shop. I can write down what they're called. I'm sure you can find a vendor online. You might even be able to buy one in Koreatown."

He sat up and grabbed a pen, and scrawled a note, chuckling to himself. Tearing the sheet off the pad, he rose and handed it across to Celeste.

"You didn't need a ruse to get in the door," he said. "I would have talked to you regardless."

She thanked him, and Truman followed her out to the street, and back to her car.

"What did you think?" Truman said as they climbed in.

"Park seems like an honest enough guy. He was happy to share his art resources. Flavio would never do that."

"I'm kind of embarrassed that we lied to him."

"You didn't know that you didn't need to," Celeste said. "At least he wasn't upset about it."

"My sense is that this guy is just a patsy. Flavio is the real crook."

"Park was definitely sanguine about being accused of fraud."

"He knows there's no point in anyone suing him for breaking copyright," Truman said. "It's a small-batch low-value product, so it's not worth the expense. He's not upset because he knows that the most we can do is ask him to stop."

"I guess that's what we just did." She started the engine. "So what's next?"

"I need to talk to Huck. Is the door closed on you going back to Eurorapt?"

"I haven't finished what they wanted me to do, so I can walk in there without arousing suspicion. But I'm a little worried that Flavio will find out I've been going through their files."

"I think you'd hear about it first, don't you? Flavio isn't the type to hold his tongue."

"Probably. But I'm not going there today—I have a client meeting at the gallery."

TWENTY-ONE

CELESTE DROPPED TRUMAN AT his place, and as he climbed the stairs, his phone buzzed in his pants. He pulled it out to find a text from Neil:

Any news for me?

He wanted to know more about what Flavio had taken from him, he knew. Truman paused on the stairs to text back:

Soon. I'll let you know.

Once he was in his loft, he sent a text to Huck:

Do you have time for me today?

A moment later his phone rang—it was Huck. "I'm working today," he said, when Truman picked up. "But can I see you tonight?"

"Do you want to go dancing?"

"Like in WeHo?" Huck said. "I always feel like the token brown guy."

"There's lots of places around here that aren't like that."

———·———

AFTER CELESTE HAD MET with her client, and she was alone again in the empty gallery, she sat at her desk to read through some paperwork. She looked up at the sound of the door opening. It was Flavio, filling the frame as he stepped inside and then closed it behind him. A flash of fear struck. He must have found out about her snooping. She sat up straighter and met his gaze.

"Will you come for dinner with me?" he said, flashing a smile.

Celeste knotted her brow. "Just me, or the whole office?"

He laughed. "Just you and me."

"Yeah ... I don't know."

"Why the chilly attitude?" Flavio said. "On the weekend we were getting along just fine."

"You seriously have to ask me that?" she demanded. "You neglected to tell me that you were exclusive with someone else."

He waved a hand. "You don't know what the terms of that relationship are."

"Alicia had a pretty clear understanding of the terms. She came over here on Sunday to fill me in."

"Come on—I'm just talking about dinner."

Celeste stifled a retort, and stood up, and grabbed her bag. "So where are we eating?"

She locked up the gallery, and climbed into the passenger side of the Jag, and Flavio drove to a place nearby. Celeste had been here, but only in the warmer months. It was in a courtyard, sheltered by the surrounding buildings, and seemed like it would be too cold to sit outside in the winter. But there were big heat lamps, she saw as they walked in, and the host put them at a table under one.

When the server stepped over, Flavio ordered a pint of beer.

"Just water for me," Celeste said.

"Oh, Celeste, come on—it's a brewpub," he said.

"I don't feel like beer right now."

They ordered food, and the server stepped away.

"So why did you need to log in to the Eurorapt cloud drive?" Flavio said.

Celeste met his eye. He was watching her closely.

"Some of the design files had components that were in locked folders." She waved a hand. "When you position one graphic inside another file, it doesn't copy the whole thing. It just inserts a thumbnail and a link to the original. I managed to compile everything once the original folders were unlocked."

"OK," he said evenly, still watching her.

The server set down their drinks, and Celeste picked up her glass.

"You don't seem convinced."

"I thought I'd moved everything. I didn't think you'd need that access."

"Well, I did." She frowned. "Why else would I ask for it?"

"I'm not sure."

"I'd say you're a suspicious person." She tapped her glass against his. "Cheers."

"You can't toast with water," he said, and took a sip of his beer. "If you're messing with me, I'm not going to let it go."

"I have to wonder about you, Flavio." She sat back and gestured vaguely. "I'm doing you a favor, working on your graphic drudgery, and then you invite me out to dinner and toss vague threats around. What exactly are you up to that you have to be so afraid? It's the way criminals think."

"I'm not a criminal," he said intently, "and I'm not threatening you." He looked away, and huffed, and sipped his beer.

———·———

TRUMAN WAITED FOR HUCK on Main Street, and when he walked up, they embraced, Huck leaning in to kiss his neck.

"There's a hopping little bar right up here," Truman said. "Club 230."

"I've never heard of it, but that's no surprise. I

don't get out much."

Truman gestured up the block, and they set off toward it. "The crowd is mostly gay guys, and it's a good mix of people."

The music was thumping when they stepped inside.

"I love it—people who look like me," Huck said, raising his voice over the bass. "I can't believe this place is so packed on a weeknight."

"It's always packed," Truman said. "Do you want me to get drinks?"

"You said we were coming here to dance."

Truman grinned and led the way farther inside, threading through the crowd to the dance floor, where they joined the writhing throng. Huck seemed to enjoy it, and let himself go, occasionally moving close and grinding against Truman. A while later, when he started to over-heat, Truman gestured toward the main room, and made his way there, and pressed his way up to the bar.

"What are you drinking?" he asked Huck.

"Get me a draft."

Leaning close to the bartender, he said, "Two shots of tequila and two smalls."

"Do you want the good stuff?" the guy said, raising his eyebrows.

"Just the applejack."

He nodded and stepped away, and once Truman had paid him, he handed one of the shots to Huck.

"Really?" Huck's brow furrowed, but he took the little glass.

"Together." Truman raised his own shot, and they both slammed them.

Huck howled at the intensity of it, his face contorting. Truman grabbed the beer glasses, and handed him one, then stepped away from the bar. A quick mouthful of beer killed the sting of the tequila, and before long he'd downed most of it.

"Do you want to go to your place?" Huck said, leaning in. "A little less stimulation might be nice."

Truman nodded and took another gulp, then set his glass down and led the way outside. Once they were on the street, Huck flapped his arms. It did feel good, Truman realized, the chill of the night air on his sweaty shirt.

"Where's the LeBaron?" Truman said.

"Redge is at home. I took a ride-share. I thought we might be drinking."

Truman briefly put an arm around his waist and gave him a squeeze, then pointed in the direction of his pad.

TWENTY-TWO

AFTER THEY'D EATEN, THE check came, and Celeste folded her arms, waiting for Flavio to pick it up. He'd asked her out, and he'd pressed the issue, so he could buy. He did take it, eventually, and paid without protest. Walking out to his car, he eyed her.

"Do you want to go somewhere quieter?"

"That's not going to happen," she said. "Not after the way Alicia reacted. She read me the riot act."

"Things aren't as simple as that."

She paused at the passenger door and met his gaze across the top of the Jag. "You can drop me at the gallery."

WHEN THEY GOT UP to Truman's loft, Huck

flopped on the purple sofa and stretched out.

"My ears are still ringing, and I'm totally buzzed from that tequila."

"It's a good buzz, though," Truman said, and lifted his legs to sit under them, and then took off Huck's shoes, and massaged his feet.

"Nice. I could get used to this."

"Why don't you have a main squeeze, anyway? A man for foot-massage duty?"

"I work a lot. It's not easy to meet guys."

"Flavio actually warned me not to get with you."

"For real?" Huck demanded. "When did you see Flavio?"

"He had me help him move a bunch of fabric and clothes on Monday. He said it was a favor, but in hindsight I think it was really just unpaid manual labor."

"What did he say about me?"

"That you needed to focus on work," Truman said, "and not on bagging a boyfriend."

"That motherfucker," he snapped. "It's like he wants me to be alone."

"I'd say that's exactly what he wants. So that you'll give all your time and energy to Eurorapt."

Huck was flushed, he saw, and his mouth was a tight line. Truman kept working on his feet, massaging his toes.

"Do you have any more booze?" he said finally.

"I've got a bottle of tequila," Truman said, "and some wine coolers."

"Let's do another shot."

Truman chuckled and got up, and took the tequila bottle from the cupboard above the fridge, and poured a half inch each into a couple of tumblers, then carried them back to the sofas.

Huck sat up and took one, and clinked it against Truman's. "Cheers." Without waiting for Truman, he slammed it, and grimaced. "It burns."

"Tequila is the best kind of burn," Truman said, and slammed his own, then shuddered involuntarily as he set the empty glass on the coffee table. He took a breath. "I was pissed at Flavio when I figured out he was just using me for labor. I know not everything Eurorapt does is on the up-and-up."

Huck scoffed. "You don't know the half of it. Flavio is a dick."

"I don't know him very well, but from what I've seen, I'd have to concur. What's the deal with the crypto exchange?"

"There is no 'exchange.'" He waggled his fingers to put air quotes around the word, then draped his arms on the back of the sofa.

"Flavio is marketing one to people. Celeste watched him give a sales pitch to one of her colleagues."

"It's bogus," he said simply. "Flavio sends statements to investors with the value of their coin, but there's no actual wallets. He's just taking their cash and their coin and putting it into Eurorapt's wallet."

Truman watched him for a moment. Why was Huck being so forthcoming right now?

"Don't people want to make withdrawals sometimes?"

"It's still new," Huck said. "So far, anyone who wants their money out of it gets excuses, or Flavio sends part of what they want and tells them there's a technical holdup with the rest."

"So it's a straight-up scam."

"It's all about trust."

"That can't go on forever." Truman waved a hand. "Someone's going to call the cops, or the Treasury Department."

"Flavio calls it the tipping point. When you've maximized investments but before the roof falls in."

"What happens then?"

"We're going to buy a beach house in Peru. I've been learning Spanish."

"Why Peru?" Truman said. "Because Flavio grew up there?"

"And they don't extradite for financial disputes."

"I kind of can't believe you're admitting all this."

Huck frowned. "I'm not going to cut you in, if that's what you mean. This is our gig."

"That's not what I meant. I don't want in on your scam."

"What, you're going to grow a conscience all of a sudden, and clutch at your pearls, and call the cops?" He laughed. "Come on, Truman. I know you. You're the same as me. I saw you steal that sushi the other night, after you'd acted like a snob with the chef."

Truman had to think about it, but he remembered the incident. "I didn't order that plate, but I paid for it. It wound up on the bill. I checked." He studied Huck's face for a moment, tried to parse his wry expression. "Snagging a plate of *kampyo* isn't really the same as what you're doing. You're stealing serious dough from people."

"Most of the value in crypto is from the rapid increase in attention it's getting," he said, waving dismissively. "It looks like it's worth more than the initial buy-in, but that's just on paper."

"But the buyers believe that value. And it is their money."

"The people holding it don't really need it," Huck said. "They're already rich."

Truman took a breath and looked away. "That doesn't mean it's not theft," he said, half to himself.

Maybe Huck knew him better than he was willing to admit. His con wasn't that different from things that Truman had done, the way he'd rationalized stealing from drug dealers. Most of that cash was still right here, across the room, hidden in his bathroom walls. There was no moral high ground in that.

"It seems to me Flavio is exploiting you," Truman said. "Acting like the boss, and telling you who you can date. He's controlling you. With Alicia it's even easier—he's sleeping with her."

"You don't understand our business. Our relationship. It's a partnership."

"What always amazes me about crooks is how they think it can't happen to them."

"You're actually calling me a crook," Huck said.

He shrugged. "It fits."

"What is it that you think is going to happen to me?"

"If Flavio is willing to rip off his crypto clients, why wouldn't he rip you off too?"

"I thought you understood this." His eyes narrowed. "We're the same, Truman."

"Hypothetically, what if Flavio makes that Peru trip on his own, and leaves you here holding the bag?"

"We're partners. There's loyalty. He'd never do that to me."

"A minute ago you were surprised to hear that he was trying to cock-block you. What if all the paperwork for Eurorapt's crypto wallet is in your name? That would imply Flavio is setting you up to take the fall. He could drain the wallet, and leave the country. You'd be left here with no money and a bunch of pissed-off investors. Fraud on that scale can put you away for twenty years."

Huck scoffed. "How could you possibly know any of that? You're just making stuff up."

"Why don't you check into it?" Truman said.

"Just in case. Make sure I'm really just making stuff up."

Huck reached for his shoes and pulled one on. "I liked you, Truman. I can't believe you're being such a dick."

"I'm not trying to be a dick. I'm trying to be real."

Pulling on his other shoe, Huck scoffed and avoided his gaze.

"You don't have to leave," Truman said, watching him tie his laces.

Ignoring that, Huck got up and walked out, pulling the door closed behind him.

Truman sat for a minute and thought it through. That had gone south fast. It was too late to phone Celeste, he decided. Instead he sent her a text:

Developments. Call me when you wake up.

———•———

AGAIN TRUMAN WOKE UP to the sound of the doorbell, and hustled over to answer. It was Celeste. When she walked in, she was wearing a tweed jacket and a cream-colored turtleneck.

"I feel like I've become your morning alarm," she said.

He went over to the counter, rubbing sleep out of his eyes, and started the espresso machine. "I had a late night. I went dancing with Huck."

Celeste grinned. "Booty call?"

"That was the plan, but he got mad and left. I kind of told him Flavio might be setting him up. That the crypto paperwork is all in his name."

"Are you kidding me?" Celeste demanded. "Why would you do that? I thought we weren't there yet."

"Flavio is taking advantage of him."

"See, this is what happens when you sleep with your targets. You lose all objectivity."

Truman sighed and filled the demitasse cups.

"You're thinking with your dick." She huffed. "Did you tell him how you know that?"

"Of course not," he said, and handed her a cup, and waved her over to the sofas.

"At least Flavio won't be gunning for me yet."

"Huck did tell me that the crypto exchange is a total scam," Truman said. "We already knew that, but he confirmed it. He said the plan is that they're going to cash out and move to Peru. No extradition, he claims."

Her brow furrowed. "Huck actually admitted that?"

"We were drinking, and he was mad at Flavio. I think he thought I'd be supportive of the whole scheme."

"He must have been pretty tight."

"Huck has this idea in his head that I'm a lowlife too," Truman said. "He thought I'd ripped off the sushi bar where we ate."

"Did you?"

"No," he said flatly.

"Truman, I was the one digging around in their files. If he runs to Flavio and tells him what you said, they'll know it was me who saw those documents." She told him about their dinner last night, and Flavio's veiled threat.

"Let's not embrace fear," Truman said. "Flavio is just a bully. Even if they put it together, and they know what we're up to, he's not going to come after you, or me. Their only sensible move would be to radically accelerate their departure. We know they've already got a ton of other people's money set aside."

Celeste sipped at her java and thought about it. "That actually makes sense. Why would he risk coming after us when we could rat them out?"

"Exactly."

"Did Huck mention a time frame for this plan?"

"He said Flavio was still collecting investors, and stalling anyone who wanted to withdraw funds."

"Once they bug out," she said, "all the clothing stuff won't matter anymore. They'll have to abandon it. Do you think it's time to call the cops?"

"Would they even believe us?"

"We've got evidence. The photos I took."

"But none of that is admissible, is it? The prosecutors would want primary sources."

"I wonder," Celeste said. "I was working for Eurorapt, and they gave me access to the files.

Maybe I'm just reporting a crime at my work-place. I might be a primary source."

"The patterns and prints are definitely stolen goods," Truman said, "but I'd wager that's not even felony-level thievery. The crypto scam defi-nitely is."

"We don't really have any evidence of that besides what Huck told you. The investors who got ripped off would have to make the complaint."

"You're right," he said. "There's no point in taking this to the cops. Does that mean we're done? I guess I should talk to Yaz today."

Celeste's phone buzzed, and she pulled it out to check. As Truman watched, she glanced at the screen, and her eyebrows shot up.

"It's Flavio," she said. "Do I answer?"

"Of course you should answer. Find out what's going on."

"No fear," she said, then picked up the call, and held out the phone so Truman could hear.

"Are you coming in today?" Flavio said, his voice rattling the phone's tinny speaker.

"I finished most of the image editing."

"There are still a dozen files here that you didn't even touch. Are you seriously going to leave me hanging?"

"I guess it won't take me that long. I'll come in later today." She ended the call and eyed Tru-man. "Maybe Huck didn't say anything."

"At least not yet." He sipped his coffee. "You're brave to walk in there."

"Like you said, he's not going to mess with me. Bullies work mostly through intimidation."

"Now that we know what they're up to, we could make sure Eurorapt can't use any more of Yaz's designs."

Celeste cracked a smile. "You mean delete all the files for Yaz's prints? The manufacturer will still have them."

"But Eurorapt won't. Yaz can go talk to Park herself and take ownership. Flavio's going to be on the beach in South America anyway."

"That's kind of brilliant."

"Let's wait to talk to Yaz until you've done it," he said.

"My one concern is that Flavio will definitely know it was me who did the deleting."

"Flavio is going to have bigger things to worry about."

TWENTY-THREE

CELESTE PARKED ON A side street, a block away from the Eurorapt office. She didn't want to be right outside the back door in case she needed to get away from there in a hurry. Walking up to the street entrance, the door was unlocked, and when she stepped inside, no one was in the front office.

Pushing her way through the door into the back room, she found Flavio at his desk, and Alicia standing nearby, a sheaf of paper in hand.

"I love that jacket," Alicia said.

"I guess I shouldn't admit that it came from a thrift store."

"You should actually boast about that." She chuckled. "Half the people in this business would have spent eight grand for the couture version."

"Huck isn't answering his phone," Flavio said.

"I wonder if Truman knows where he is? They were going to meet up last night."

"I'm sure he's awake by now," Celeste said. "You can call him."

"Can you do it? I'm not sure he'll pick up for me."

She frowned but dug out her phone and sent Truman a text:

> Flavio is worried that Huck isn't answering his phone. Any news from him?

Flavio got up and waved to his chair as he went to the cutting table, and leaned over it, bracing himself with his hands, studying something on the tabletop. Celeste sat at the desk, and took hold of the mouse, and fired up the design software. When her phone buzzed, she glanced at it to see Truman's reply:

> Nada since he left here in a snit.

"Truman hasn't seen him since last night," Celeste called to him.

Flavio didn't respond, his expression clouding. He stood erect and eyed Alicia, sitting at her desk now.

"Did he sleep at Truman's?" Alicia said.

"He didn't say. Do you want me to ask?"

"Don't bother," Flavio said, and walked to the door to the alley, stepping out and closing it behind him. Alicia watched him leave, then looked at Celeste.

"What else did Truman say?"

"Nothing," Celeste said. "Just that they went out last night."

On the desktop, Alicia's phone rang, and she picked it up to check. She held it to her ear to answer, and got involved in a conversation, something about garment production. Celeste tuned her out and focused on the computer screen.

Next was a test of how paranoid Flavio really was. She clicked on the cloud drive folder, and the familiar security prompt came up. She typed in the password Alicia had used the other day: WEREFAMOUS. It worked—the folder opened to reveal its contents. Despite his concern about her motives, Flavio hadn't changed it. She grinned to herself. Big mistake.

She quickly found the folder with Yaz's designs in it. In the web browser she spent a minute downloading several photos of kittens, then gave them the same file names as Yaz's print designs, and copied them over the design files. It took longer to find the previous versions of the files and to delete all of them, and then wipe them from the trash folder, but eventually it looked like she'd erased any trace of Yaz's work.

Celeste should probably do the same for all these designers. Like Yaz, they'd been ripped off by these lowlifes. But Yaz was the priority, as she was Truman's client, and would presumably be paying him. If Celeste interfered too much, they might twig sooner to what she'd done.

Clicking open one of the outstanding images that Flavio wanted her to sanitize, she stared at it for a moment, zooming in on the designer's logo. She couldn't do it, she decided. Enough with enabling the piracy.

After she'd closed all the folders and the software, she locked the screen and got up. Alicia was still on the phone, listening and occasionally interjecting an "Uh-huh." She eyed Celeste, raising her eyebrows, a tacit query.

"Bye," Celeste said, under her breath, and waved as she went into the front office, then walked out to the street.

On the way to her car, Celeste pulled out her phone and called Yaz.

"Do you have a minute to meet today?" she said, when Yaz picked up.

"There's news?"

"Lots. Can you come over to Truman's place?"

A few minutes later Celeste rolled up at his loft, and climbed out, and rang the bell. When she got upstairs, Truman was waiting at the door.

"You nuked the files?"

"I did what I could. I hope they're completely gone."

Truman beamed. "Right on."

"Yaz is on her way over."

"It's definitely time to fill her in."

Celeste took an Italian soda from the fridge, and told him about her morning at Eurorapt. Before long the door buzzed, and Truman went over to answer.

"Come on up," he shouted at the machine, and pressed the button to unlock it.

Yaz was wearing her hair up in a messy bundle, and a denim jacket with a red scarf, and chunky thick boots. A canvas satchel was slung over one shoulder.

After they exchanged greetings, Truman said, "Do you want an espresso, or a soda?"

"No thanks." Yaz eyed Celeste. "So what did you find out?"

"You hired Truman," she said. "He's the one who should fill you in. Let's sit."

"We both worked on it," Truman said, following them to the sofas. "Celeste has mad detective skills."

As she sat down, Yaz gestured impatiently for him to continue.

"The guy who stole your design is named Flavio," he said. "He runs a company called Eurorapt."

Yaz waved a hand. "I've never heard of it."

"They've ripped off lots of people in the industry. It's their business model."

"This guy got hold of my look book?"

"He got it directly from your computer," Celeste said. "He had the design file."

"Bloody hell."

"How do you think Flavio got into your computer?" Truman said. "He also shills cryptocurrency. Did you ever talk to anyone in the industry about that?"

Her brow furrowed. "My old roommate was all technical. Harold. He talked a lot about crypto."

"Could he have known how to log into your machine?"

"I know he had my password. He used to fix my computer. He's not around anymore, though. Things ended poorly. He still owes me money."

"There it is," Celeste said. "He must have copied your work and sold it to Flavio."

"If he's a tech guy, you might have to do more than just change your password," Truman said. "He might have a backdoor to get into your system. You should take it to a professional to check."

"That stupid little fuck," Yaz said. "I thought I was done with him. So how can I go after this Flavio guy?"

Truman grinned. "Celeste already did."

"I went to work in his office," Celeste said. "I got into his files, and deleted everything related to you."

"Girl," she said emphatically. "You rock. How much of my stuff did he have?"

"There were four files, all of them print designs. One of them was that beautiful paisley."

"I know exactly when they were copied, then. It would have been when Harold was moving out."

"The company that made that bolt of fabric is a manufacturer with an office near here," Truman said. "I'm thinking you can go in and talk to the owner. He's a man named Park. You can explain that Flavio pirated your work."

"Flavio can easily deny that," she said.

"He's not going to be in the picture for much longer," Truman said. "I can't get into the details as to why."

"Tell Park that you won't sue him if he lets you take over the project," Celeste said. "We talked to him. He's a reasonable person. Knowing that he inadvertently ripped you off might make him amenable to discounting the production costs of another one of your prints."

Yaz nodded. "I'm amazed that you figured it out." She asked a few more questions, and eventually sat back, and took a breath. "So what do I owe you?"

"How about two grand?" Truman said. "That's what we talked about up front."

"That seems very reasonable," Yaz said. "I thought it might be a lot more. You've been at it over a week."

"Well, I didn't work on it nonstop."

"I brought cash," she said, and flipped open her satchel. Once she'd counted out a stack of C-notes, and handed it over, she rose, and held Truman's gaze. "Thanks for your help."

After she'd gone, Celeste grinned at him.

"You let her off cheap."

"I know she's not wealthy, so it was the friends and family discount." He split the bundle, handing a sheaf of the bills to her. "Half of this is yours."

"Dollar, dollar bill, y'all," she said, and grinned

as she tucked it away. "Thanks."

"Thank yourself. You did as much as I did."

Truman's phone buzzed, and he pulled it out to look. "This is Neil. I should take it."

When he picked up, Neil's voice was strained.

"Flavio has been on my case today," he said. "He really wants me to transfer my coin holdings to him."

"Don't do it," Truman said. "You know why."

"Can we talk about this, at least? I'm feeling a lot of pressure."

"Not on the phone. I'm at my place. Come over here and we'll talk."

Once he'd ended the call, Celeste said, "Why not on the phone? You think he's taping you?"

"Or sitting there with Flavio."

"Seriously?" she demanded. "You're the one who said we weren't going to embrace fear."

"It's not very likely, right? Still, it's safer to talk to him here. Biff says never spill the beans when you're on the horn—those cheap dames down at the exchange are always listening in, and they'll sell you out to a mug at a dance hall for the big eye and a watered-down cocktail."

"Such sage advice for our era," Celeste said, waving a hand. "It's almost like no time has passed at all."

"Do you want to stay for this meet? He'll be here soon."

"I'm thinking I should go to the gallery."

"I'd rather you didn't," he said. "If you're here,

I won't be tempted to sleep with him."

"The other option is just to say no."

"You make it sound so much easier than it actually is."

She nodded to the coffee machine. "At least fix me up with some java while we're waiting."

Truman went over and made espresso, and handed her a little cup, and savored his own. He started at the sound of the door buzzer.

"Go time," he muttered, and went over to answer. Once he'd heard Neil's familiar voice through the static, he buzzed him up.

Neil was wearing basic jeans and a black turtleneck, again with the thick-rimmed eyeglasses.

"This is my operative," Truman said as he came in, gesturing to Celeste.

"You can call me Celeste."

"Neil Nephard," he said, and made a little bow from the neck.

"Your reputation precedes you," she said.

He beamed. "What a lovely thing to say."

"Do you want a coffee?" Truman said.

Neil shook his head. "I'm already jittery enough."

He waved to the sofas, and the three of them sat down.

"There's no crypto exchange," Truman said, leaning toward Neil. "It's just Flavio taking people's holdings and issuing bogus receipts."

Neil waved a hand. "What evidence do you have of that?"

"I interviewed one of the staff. Eurorapt has only one cryptocurrency wallet. It's not an exchange. Some of the clients haven't been able to get their funds out again. That's because Flavio is never going to give them back."

Celeste eyed him. Truman easily could have explained about the banking documents she'd found, but he hadn't. He was leaving it up to her whether she wanted to implicate herself in the skulduggery.

Neil sighed. "I'm not saying that I don't believe you, but so far it just sounds like a story. For all I know you're the ones running the con."

"In Flavio's files there were documents from your company," Celeste said, holding his gaze. "Patterns for a couple swimsuits and some print designs. Let me show you."

She pulled out her phone and tapped at it, then handed it to Neil. Truman rose and sat beside Neil, draping an arm behind him on the back of the sofa and leaning in to look at the little screen. It was a photo of a computer monitor, with the software controls visible along the bottom, and filling the screen was a yellow-and-orange design of overlapping stars and twisting ribbons.

"Oh, god," Neil muttered. "That's mine."

"Look through them," Celeste said. "There's more."

He swiped through several images, his brow furrowing. "No one has seen this collection yet. I just created it."

"And yet it's on Flavio's computer."

"So it's true. They've stolen from me." Neil handed her the phone. "How did you get into Flavio's files?"

Celeste waved a hand. "All I can say is that it came up in the course of the investigation."

"Another hard-nosed detective," Neil said, raising his eyebrows. "That print hasn't even gone to the manufacturer yet."

"I assume Flavio plans to race you to market," Truman said. "He has all the design files."

"He can't," Neil said, raising his voice. "That's my intellectual property."

"How did they get it from you?" Celeste said.

"Truman knows." He frowned and glanced at him sidelong. "He had me change my password."

"I had a suspicion," Truman said. "I didn't have direct evidence until Celeste saw it."

"He tricked me." Neil rubbed his eyes. "I'm so stupid. A sucker for a pretty face."

"It happens to lots of people," Truman said. "Otherwise there'd be no point in running a con."

"They didn't just target you," Celeste said. "Eurorapt pilfered the work of a dozen other designers."

"How does the cryptocurrency fit into it?"

"They used that as an excuse to get access to computers and cloud drives and bank accounts," Truman said. "They asked people to give them login credentials to set up some kind of crypto software. I'm sure it doesn't even exist. At some point the crypto scam must have become more lucrative, so the fashion knock-offs were relegated to a side hustle."

"Obviously I'm going to talk to the police about this," Neil said, and eyed Celeste. "But there won't be anything for them to act on without a statement from you."

"Of course—I'll be happy to talk to them." She dug in her bag, and pulled out a business card, and handed it to him.

Neil eyed it for a moment. "Are you a gallerist for real, or is that a cover for your detective operations?"

She had to smile. "It's my real job."

"Your willingness to talk to the police makes me think you didn't do anything illegal to obtain those photos," Neil said, and pocketed the card.

"I was working for Eurorapt, and they gave me access to their files," Celeste said. "I'm sure they'd rather I hadn't gone snooping, but nothing about it was illegal."

When she glanced at Truman, he had a smile on his face. Impressed that she was willing to go that far, maybe. They both knew getting involved with the police or the district attorney's office meant a world of pain—interviews and statements and depositions, stupid subpoenas and more questions, like being frog-marched through an irrational byzantine labyrinth.

"Flavio's a crook," she said, and shrugged. "Someone needs to shut him down."

"Is there anything else that Huck might have obtained access to?" Truman said, eyeing Neil. "You should change your other passwords, or your codes, or whatever you need to do."

Neil frowned and waved dismissively. "OK, Truman, I get it. I'll get to work." He got up and headed toward the door, pausing briefly to turn to Celeste. "It was a pleasure to meet you."

Once he'd walked out, and Truman had closed the door, Celeste said, "I guess he finally believes you."

"He's not big on the thank-yous, though."

"I'm sure he feels like a sucker. If I were him I'd be pretty freaked out right now. Besides, you're not in this for the gratitude. You already got paid."

"Good point. Do you want to go blow some of that sweet cash? I'm feeling flush."

"Tonight," she said. "I should get to the gallery. I've been slacking."

After she'd left, Truman spent some time at his desk, with his laptop, making notes about the case. Writing about what Huck had told him, he wondered if he'd had time to cool off. He dug out his phone and sent him a text:

Sorry I upset you last night. Can we hang out?

Truman was immersed in his writing again when Huck's reply came:

I'm really busy right now.

That seemed odd. Whatever he was doing,

Flavio obviously hadn't been aware of it this morning when he was trying to track him down. Truman sent another text:

> You know Flavio and Alicia are looking for you, right?

A minute later he followed up with another message:

> They can't figure out why you're not answering your phone.

But there was no response from Huck.

TWENTY-FOUR

THE GALLERY WAS DEAD quiet, as usual, although Saffron was in today, up in her office. Celeste got settled and started reading some blog posts about what was happening in the local art scene.

The calm silence was broken when the front door swung open, and Flavio walked in. He looked pale, his eyes sharp, and sweat beaded his brow.

"Hey, big guy," Celeste said, sitting back in her chair. "I finished up everything I could with those files this morning. I can't really do much more to them."

He stood in front of her desk, staring at her. "I'm missing six million bucks of other people's money."

"Wow. That does not sound optimal."

"What do you know about it?"

She frowned. "I'm not your accountant."

"You had access to my cloud files," he shouted, waving his arms.

"So did your coconspirators. Your girlfriend with the grudge is the one who gave me access, remember? Then there's the guy you treat like a lackey. It sounds like they beat you to the big cash grab."

"Damn it," he snapped. "I knew I couldn't trust you."

"I didn't touch your money, Flavio."

"Prove it."

She scoffed. "If I suddenly had six million bucks, I would not be sitting here."

He stepped closer to her desk. "So what happened?"

"How the hell should I know?" Looking him over, she saw that his fists were balled. "You seem agitated. Just to be clear, there are cameras all over this place." She pointed one out, near the ceiling behind her desk, and then another in the corner.

Saffron descended the blue stairs, her heels clanking on the metal treads. She was wearing a chic tan pantsuit, a cherry-red briefcase dangling from one hand. As she stepped onto the floor, she eyed Flavio.

"Well, hello there."

Flavio glared at her for a moment, then scoffed and stormed out, the door slamming as he left.

"Did you actually rob him?" Saffron said,

turning to Celeste and raising an eyebrow.

"Of course not."

"He looked upset."

"You don't need to worry about him. He won't be back here." Celeste dug out her phone. "I need to call Truman."

"I should have known it had something to do with that little twinkie," Saffron said, languorously waving a hand. "You know, he's like an actual gas-station snack. He seems so sweet at first, but then you wind up with a toothache."

Ignoring her, Celeste spoke to Truman when he picked up. "Flavio was just here. He's freaking out. Can you come over?"

Once she'd ended the call, Saffron said, "This is a place of business. No drama."

Celeste met her gaze. "You love the excitement, Saffron. You know you do. Don't even try to convince me otherwise. And I know you can handle people like Flavio. I've seen you do it."

"Fair enough." She chuckled. "Maybe there's a satisfying frisson in just a little bit of drama. Anyway, I've got a meeting. Ciao, darling."

Saffron went out the back way, to the alley where she parked her obnoxiously expensive SUV. Once she heard the fire door slam, and she was alone, Celeste took a breath. Her heart was still pounding. Glancing at the front door, she briefly considered locking it, but rationally, she knew Flavio wouldn't be coming back. She dug in her bag and found a Xanax, and bit off half the tab, and crunched it between her teeth.

"So what did Flavio say, exactly?" Truman said, as he stepped in the door a few minutes later. He was out of breath, and sweaty, like he'd hustled to get here.

"That someone took six million dollars from him."

"That's how much was in the crypto wallet."

"The wallet that's in Huck's name," Celeste said. "Huck being the guy Alicia and Flavio couldn't track down this morning."

"I tried to talk to him," Truman said, and dropped into the chair in front of her desk, running a hand through his hair and taking deep breaths. "He said he was busy, and then I thought he'd ghosted me."

"Do you think he drained the crypto wallet?"

"I know he did. I got a message from him a few minutes ago." He pulled out his phone, and tapped at it, and handed it across to her.

Celeste spent a minute reading the lengthy text:

> Hey, Truman—you were right about the paperwork. Thanks for thinking of that. It's all in my name, so I figured, why not just take it? Better than waiting around to be the fall guy. All the transactions have cleared, and I'm in the air now. I won't be back. Anyway, I left Redge in Lot C at LAX. The keys are under the mat, and the title is in the glove box. I signed him over to you. Don't leave him there too long—that place costs a fortune.

"Redge is his car?" Celeste said, looking up at him and handing the phone back.

"I guess it's my car now."

"So Huck cleaned them out," she said. "That little weasel."

"It sounds like he's on his way to Peru right now."

"I bet he picked a different nonextradition country. One that Flavio wouldn't be likely to visit."

"It's completely my fault," Truman said, his brow furrowing. "I tipped him off, which means I helped him rob all of Flavio's investors."

"Careful, now." Celeste's eyes narrowed. "Did you tell him what you told him with this outcome in mind?"

"Of course not. But why didn't I anticipate that he might flee? I'm not supposed to be the chump."

"So you made a mistake, but you didn't do it on purpose. And it's a mistake that's not fixable. That means you have to ditch your guilt and move on."

"But I feel like an ass. That car is the proceeds of a crime."

"It's just a car. Listen, Truman," she said intently. "Think about it. You can't tell the cops any of this. Not that we knew about the exchange, not what you told Huck. They'll charge us both as accessories."

"Neil is going to drop us in the middle of it regardless. You gave him your card."

"Our story has to be limited to the fashion stuff. That's all I saw in Eurorapt's cloud drive. Your man Biff says, 'Play your cards close to the vest.' I'm so glad you did that with Neil—we didn't tell him anything about finding the crypto documentation."

"I get it." Truman waved helplessly. "We lie all the time, right? In the big picture it's a tiny omission."

"Exactly. From now on, we're not even going to discuss that part of it." Celeste glanced up at the security camera over her desk, then swiveled to her keyboard. "I'm going to delete the last few minutes of our conversation. Then there won't be any record of this anywhere."

"It's also possible that Neil's complaint won't be a priority for the investigators," Truman said, watching her work. "Once the people Flavio scammed out of big money go after him, that'll be the focus."

"You know you're going to get deposed regardless. Once Flavio is in the spotlight, they're going to want to know what we know." Once she'd deleted the files, Celeste paused the recording and turned back to him, concern in her eyes. "I took a bunch of photos of the crypto documents on Eurorapt's computer."

"Delete those," Truman said. "Like, now."

She huffed and pulled out her phone, tapping through the images and trashing them, then emptied the trash folder. "There's still copies of them somewhere," she said. "All they'd have to do is subpoena my cloud storage."

"If we keep our mouths shut, no one is ever going to know they should do that."

Celeste nodded. "What about that text from Huck? The cops will go all forensic on his phone account."

"I don't think they'll find it—the message didn't come from Huck's number. He must have bought a new phone. I'd bet cash money it's a prepaid one that's not connected to his identity."

"Clever fellow." Celeste took a breath. "Delete that message, yeah?"

Truman looked at his phone and tapped at it, then deleted Huck's new number as well. "And that's the end of it."

"The end of what?" Celeste frowned. "I don't know what you're talking about."

"Me either." In his hand his phone buzzed, and he picked it up to glance at it. "I just got a text from Neil." He swiped at the screen. "A chatty text from Neil."

"Read it to me," she said. "Unless it's mushy."

"He says, 'I realize I forgot my manners when we spoke today. My accountant instructed me to thank you. Your intervention potentially saved me a sizable amount of money. As a token of my appreciation, I'm sending you one bitcoin.'" Truman tucked his phone away. "I'm glad he figured that out. A little expression of gratitude is mollifying."

"He must mean *some* bitcoin. A fraction of one."

"I think it's a whole one. He said 'one.'"

She threw up her hands. "Do you know what one bitcoin is worth?"

"Zero," he said flatly. "It's not really a currency. It doesn't have a government or an army behind it, so the real value of unregulated coin products is zero. One of the analysts I read said the whole thing is going to collapse at some point. At least Yaz paid me in real currency. Plus I got a ratchet car that's older than I am."

"Truman, you weirdo—gold and diamonds aren't currency either, but they have value because people are willing to trade them for greenbacks." She turned to her computer and tapped at the keyboard. "If you converted it to dollars today, one bitcoin is worth about sixty grand. You need to turn that into cash money, pronto."

"Sixty grand?" Truman demanded. "For real?"

"I'd say Neil was pretty damn grateful."

———·———